SASQUATCH SPECTRE

A *Stalk* Adventure

P. J. Hafner

Birchbark Publishing

Publisher's Cataloging in Publication

Hafner, P. J.
Sasquatch Spectre / P. J. Hafner
p.   cm.
ISBN-13: 978-06923233-1-1
1. Mystery / Suspense – Fiction   2. Florida – Fiction
I. Title

As soon as there is life, there is danger.

– Ralph Waldo Emerson

1

Cynthia Kresswell walked another three feet through the cluster of palmetto fronds. For the duration of her young life, she would take only 17 more steps.

Cynthia looked down at her smartphone. The screen with its light pink background revealed a lack of activity. No incoming texts, no calls. No contact from the bastard. *Prick.*

The evening's gloaming was overtaking the ability to see with clarity. Things were getting darker, shadows creeping in among the weeds, leaves, and stands of massive cypress trees. It was hard to tell actual moving shapes from dark globs of shadow. The snakes would start to move in earnest soon, Cynthia knew. As would the alligators. The latter usually kept to the water, but an alligator could also scamper on land like a sprinting halfback. That is, if it had a reason to. Come to think of it, a young woman walking alone in the dark, not far from the water's edge, could in fact be a reason. Kind of scary.

Thanks, Tyrell. The guy was nowhere to be found. He was probably with that tramp…never mind that the tramp was his actual girlfriend, and that Cynthia was the interloper. Cynthia's thought on the situation? *Tough.* All's fair, especially at their age. The period just out of high school was time to set the tone and establish crucial connections. Including a partner *with* connections.

Tyrell Oldham was a starting defensive back on the local community college's football team, and there was a chance he'd transfer next year to Florida State to play. If they'd have him. Tyrell was certain they would.

If that was the case, *Cynthia* had to have him. Successful, plus a tough and sexy dude. Hey, a "three-fer." Her anticipation for the meetup increased a little more with the thought.

Despite the uptick in her enthusiasm, the mood wasn't really set for romance on this November evening. Not even here, in Cayman Park. They still called it a *park*? In Cynthia's mind, it was essentially just an overgrown gateway to a patch of swampland. Tyrell had insisted it was a great spot for meeting in clandestine fashion. Go figure.

The musty blanket of Northern Florida's smells and humidity surrounded Cynthia, discouraging and repulsing her. The sooner she could leave, the better. But considering what was at stake – the ideal guy – she'd stick it out, stick to the plan. Meet Tyrell back at the old gazebo, the one covered with Spanish moss and rarely visited by locals. Forgotten. That was partly the point of meeting there, back in the park reserve's dark greenery.

She looked left, then right, and seeing no movement – and no Tyrell – shuffled a short distance closer to the gazebo's location. Just get a direct look at the old rotting structure, see if lover boy had already arrived, and if not, get the hell out of here. Why couldn't Tyrell have arranged for this rendezvous to be at a spot in the mall or something?

If he stood her up, even this once, Cynthia would say forget it from here on in. Tyrell was a player in more ways than one, and prided himself in it. He might be a catch, but she knew there were so many other fish, and life was just too short for such B.S. But what if things worked out between them? Worth the risk, for sure. Almost worth being out in this soggy wetland.

On second thought, what if this had been Tyrell's idea of a cruel joke? If he had truly wanted her to buzz off and get lost, and simply took the opportunity to lure her to this place. To the park by the swamp, so she could look around in the leafy darkness for someone who wasn't there. *Ha ha.* His way of sending a message? She knew he had it in him. If that's what was going on here, it was certainly over between them. And so much for Tyrell's claim that he only had eyes for her.

Unbeknownst to Cynthia, a different set of eyes, not those of the charismatic Tyrell, currently watched. Tyrell may no longer have had eyes only for her, but something else did. Clueless to the presence of those eyes, she moved a few more paces forward.

Then she spotted the cap. In the dimming light, Cynthia had to bend closer to it to study the baseball hat's design. From a standing position the style looked familiar to her, but it had been hard to know for sure. After crouching nearer to it, she saw the logo clearly. And recognized it immediately.

A cap from Chicola Community College. With its mascot, the bull shark, embroidered on the front. A design she had been around her whole life, growing up and still living in her home town of Chicola, Florida. Her neighborhood was just a few miles from the school. It was a popular college, one whose shirts, jackets, and caps were worn by students current and former. And by the school's jocks, especially those playing their two top sports: basketball and football. And she knew her favorite player ever, Tyrell, wore one. All the time.

Cynthia straightened up, a small quaking of distress now in the pit of her stomach. Was that Tyrell's baseball cap? If so, where was he? It could be anyone's, really. No need to worry, she insisted to herself, knowing even as she thought it the idea was nonsense. She knew the cap was Tyrell's. Absolutely knew it.

And he wasn't with it.

Cynthia wanted to call out, summon Tyrell from the darkness, but her throat was seizing up. Something was not right. Some kind of danger was looming, she could feel it. Instead of turning and hurrying away, like primitive instincts urged her to do, she opted for what most Americans under 60 now turn to in times of distress. And in times of stress. And loneliness. And boredom. And in response to just about every other emotion.

She turned to her smartphone. Holding the little pink screen in front of her eyes, her unconscious wish was that it would make things clear, straighten this misunderstanding out...provide answers.

Nope. The phone's inbox provided a big zero. No calls, no texts. No message from Tyrell. She thought for an instant of awful possibilities, of his hat lying discarded on the grass of this steamy park. And just as the ground in front of her reverberated with a thud, she'd started to consider fleeing, escaping doom.

Too late.

Cynthia lowered the phone, the lit-up screen making her reduced vision in the dark even worse. She stared straight ahead, saw nothing, then angled her gaze down a foot or so.

A massive shape had materialized in front of her. Wide, low, hulking, close to the ground. Until it stood up.

As the shape unfurled before her, she saw two massive, lengthy arms, dense and bowed legs, the outline of a wide, lowered head glaring at her from between thick shoulders. The outline of the thing suggested plenty of fur. It made no sound. She tilted her head up to follow the ascent of the shape as it arose, her own face contorting its delicate features into a terrified, misshapen grimace.

An expression Tyrell would have found quite unattractive, if he had still been living. But he was already piled up nearby, dead. Mercifully, Cynthia didn't know that, and never would. She froze in place.

In the movies, the endangered heroine cowers and screams. And screams. Sadly for Cynthia, she had time for nothing more than an anguished, constricted sound to escape from within her.

Eeee, was all she managed to squeak out. The creature then ended her anguish.

With the speed of a cobra's strike, its left arm burst toward her head, and its left fist thundered into Cynthia's temple. The blow had none of a trained boxer's science, but it contained all of the force and twice the ferocity. The strike was not meant to knock her out; it was meant to kill her. The young woman's small body collapsed to the forest floor below. The creature followed her down, administering several more clubbing blows. Both rights and lefts, slamming down like sledge hammers onto her face and skull. It then scooped up her head and slammed it into the ground. The creature put most of its weight behind the thrust.

Cynthia's brain was irreversibly damaged from the smashing fists, then extinguished completely from the thump into the earth. The creature stood up and listened; no other motion could be detected in the surrounding brush. No other people on the way. Not for now, anyway. The creature then crouched near Cynthia's body. Listening some more, this time to her. The prey's breathing had stopped, which was the main objective. With that accomplished, the massive animal moved on to its secondary objective.

While squatting and supporting some of its weight with one arm and the knuckles of one fist, the creature used its free hand to lift the girl's head, scooping it from the rear and cupping it by the ear on the opposite side. It then opened its mouth as wide as it could, exposing four large fangs: two on the top row, two on the bottom. It pulled the still-warm head toward its mouth, and thrust all four fangs, dagger-like in their sharpness, through the victim's skull.

Soon after, the creature moved off into the thickness of the forest, leaving the bodies behind. It maneuvered in silence and without fear by the water's edge, and then through the shoreline's border of dense brush. The cypress trees towering overhead obliterated any remaining sunlight, cloaking in darkness both the living and dead below.

2

Okay, you can have it, he thought. *Bitch.*

He flipped the plastic fork upwards and outwards, and the last pink popcorn shrimp became airborne.

The blonde dog inched forward, and with a pop of elongated jaws, white teeth glinting in the sun, made the little shrimp disappear. She ran her tongue along her lower lip, looked at her master, and waited for another.

Lee Bodkin returned the wolf dog's gaze, let out a sigh, and studied the blue ocean water again.

"Nothing but celery and shredded carrots left, hungry mutt," he said to it. "No shrimp. You just ate your fifth one."

Sheba, with her fluffy yellow-white fur waving in the salty breeze, stared at Bodkin. The dog displayed little emotion. She wanted another shrimp; carrots and celery just wouldn't suffice. Neither would dog food. Bodkin had presented the canine with a bowl of nuggets before heading down here to the water's edge. Sheba had crunched a few ounces of it, then let the rest sit. Dog food? Sheba chose to save her appetite. She knew a stash of Asian cuisine lurked nearby.

"And I myself only had four," Bodkin continued. He tried to look dismayed, but Sheba wasn't buying it. His dog's manipulation had worked on him again. But all in all he hadn't done too bad with his late breakfast. From the near-empty container of leftovers he'd just consumed what felt like several pounds of rice and vegetables, delicately spiced and copiously oiled.

The tasty food had come from the House of Zheng, one of only a handful of restaurants here in the oceanfront town of Chicola. The scant number of eateries shouldn't be a problem, Bodkin figured. He had seen small vacation towns with fewer, but had always managed to uncover a good feast or two. The assortment of cafes in Chicola would actually be perfect for the six nights he had booked at the Sea Foam Inn. He counted maybe eight places to eat as he drove in late last night – well, technically early this morning.

The owner of the House of Zheng, whose embroidered name insignia said *Tang*, charged him an extra dollar to reopen the grill and get out the pan and utensils. They normally closed at midnight, and Bodkin had arrived just after 1:00 AM while the restaurant crew was finishing up. Bodkin agreed to the surcharge, and after receiving the heavy container of hot food, tipped Tang with a five for his trouble.

Bodkin had just finished up a lengthy and rough assignment a couple of days earlier. Just north of Green Bay, Wisconsin, out in the woods like usual. During this time of year it was pretty frosty in those parts. That sucked after the first few days, and hypothermia soon flirted in the background.

But the bright side was obvious. He and his partner Gladdis were still alive, Sheba – attack dog, tracker, moocher of leftovers – remained intact, and the bad guys were vanquished. Plus they'd be getting another paycheck, this time from the U.S. Marshalls Service. Overall, it had been a pretty nice deal. Especially once the mission was done.

But unexpected snafus had thrown him off and sent the project askew, making things take longer than expected. That resulted in a late departure from the Minneapolis area, and led to a portion of the road trip veering into the wee hours. On a lack of sleep. Driving in a delirium was always an adventure. Sometimes a vacation could be more taxing than working.

After last night, Bodkin was now operating with a whopping five hours of sleep under his belt. Yep, five…again. For some reason, he didn't quite feel refreshed. He preferred seven hours, maybe nine when he could get it. Over the last four days, he'd had maybe 23 hours of actual z's. That was almost six hours a night. Almost. Not quite an ideal milestone in a sleep lab, perhaps, but better than, say, only four hours a night. He'd done that four-hour routine in the past too, when necessary. As well as operating on three.

In any event, Bodkin was in Florida now, sunglasses and trunks on, ready to thaw out. He figured he could rest up while soaking in the sun, absorbing the rays for some Vitamin D enhancement while the REMs kicked in.

The section of beach where Bodkin now reclined sat just a short drive southwest of Tallahassee. That route to the gulf brought a traveler to the quiet and formerly touristy town of Chicola, whose white sugar beaches overlooked the peaceful water. Sunny, calming, soothing.

Yet mostly forgotten by the bulk of America, and even more so by the rest of the vacationing world. With competition from the Miami, Daytona, and Tampa area beaches to draw tourists away, the Florida Panhandle's sand and water remained comparatively quiet. It was now months from the spring break madness, and only rare sightings of visitors occurred at distant points up and down the beach. In his state of fatigue and a body full of aches, the placid setting worked for Bodkin.

Splayed out on a plastic lounge chair, borrowed from his hotel's patio section, Bodkin surveyed the waves. It would hit 71 degrees today; at the current time, it was a sunny 67. He understood that locals thought the weather was chilly. With the weather of his home region today topping at around 18, Bodkin felt the climate to be simply balmy. Comfort was all relative.

He settled into the brittle lawn chair, and took a look at his dog. Sheba was now down on her belly, surveying the sand nearby, taking in the multitude of scents delivered by the warm winds. Looking relaxed, bored, and deadly all at the same time. She took one last gaze at the ocean, then put her head down on her paws, relaxing her body in preparation for some sunny weather shuteye. Bodkin silently agreed with her: perfect idea.

He leaned back and closed his eyes. The temperature felt as if it had inched up one degree or so, further warming his bare upper body.

Ah. Keep going, baby. Just a little warmer, just a little more steamy, humid breeze. Some more sun. Some more sleep, finally. Sun. Sleep. Sun. Sleep.

Bodkin didn't believe he was falling asleep quite yet, but gentle twitches in one arm and one leg suggested otherwise. Bliss, an emotion Bodkin rarely felt except with his partner Lita, started to saunter into his mind. More twitches. Asleep? Not quite.

Twitch.

Well, maybe.

"That animal needs to be on a leash."

Weird start for a dream.

"Sir, please restrain your animal."

Bodkin opened his eyes. Sheba had popped up from the sand to her feet. She'd made no sound doing so. His dog, half Russian Borzoi, half wolf, wasn't a barker. Pretty much just a tracker and a killer. In character, she had something behind him locked with a stare. Sheba remained calm, but intent.

Bodkin's eyes glanced at her back, at the fur there specifically. He noted that it wasn't standing on end, as it did in genuinely dire situations, and just before vicious confrontations. So far so good, in that respect at least. Sheba could always sense animosity and evil. It hadn't appeared here now. So it probably wasn't an assailant hunting down Bodkin in a quest for revenge. Good. A few of those were out there still.

But what about his nap? Dammit.

He sat up and started to look back, while slithering his hand down to the backpack next to his chair. He nudged open the top of it three inches or so, in order to reach inside quickly if warranted. A stout, stainless steel .357 magnum rested at the bottom of the pack. Along with the pistol and its six bullets, a heavily used, frequently sharpened fish fillet knife waited inside.

Both tools were nestled up next to a paper napkin, bundled into a bunch. Inside the napkin sat four oatmeal cookies; the hotel had them out for guests in the morning, with a request to "please take only one." But Bodkin had lifted a few extra. He needed nourishment to recover from his recent outing, after all. They were to be consumed after Sheba fell asleep, in order for Bodkin to have them all to himself.

This voice behind them was screwing that plan up, just like it was his elusive nap.

Bodkin removed his Costa Del Mar sunglasses and turned fully to take a look. The man standing there wore a gun on his hip, but immediately Bodkin concluded that there was a lack of danger.

The guy was a cop, or at least his fading uniform resembled what a cop would wear. Skinny guy, about 6'1", right around an inch taller than Bodkin himself. Light-colored hair, halfway between brown and blond. A simple, dated handgun rested on his hip in a worn leather holster. Appeared to be a .38 service revolver, similar to those used by most departments in the old days. Maybe just a .32 caliber, for that matter. Neither pistol design meant heavy artillery, and neither was trendy with modern police forces. But Bodkin knew – from experience – that in the right hands, the classic, boring service revolver of yesteryear was definitely still a gun. You couldn't base conclusions of deadliness on caliber or appearance. Bodkin continued to calmly appraise the man.

Carrying a gun or no, an apparent lack of confidence swirled about the guy. He looked at Bodkin, then at Sheba, then down at the sand, then out to the water. Then back to Bodkin, then down to his own feet.

"Leash required; county rules," said the man in uniform. He pursed his lips and nodded to Bodkin, as if to confirm the thought.

"Understandable," Bodkin said. "With all the swimmers and sun bathers around, imagine the harassment of beachgoers that could result."

The man in uniform looked east along the shore, then west. Currently just one dog and two people, counting Sheba, Bodkin, and himself. He looked over to Bodkin again, who now grinned back. The all-for-fun grin, not the "got ya" grin. Keep things running smoothly, Bodkin figured. For now anyway. After all, this was supposed to be a reprieve from his normal life, and all the excitement, misery, and confrontation it included. No need to provoke. Plus, the man in their presence just didn't have the feel of anxiety or look of anticipation a hitman normally does before action. Probably safe to cooperate with the stranger.

So to prove his willingness to cooperate, Bodkin looked away from the uniformed guy and back out to the sea. He reached his right arm out toward Sheba, and snapped his fingers. The wolf dog's formerly aloof behavior, such as when she was recently angling for food morsels, changed in abrupt fashion. To her the finger snap, as with other master-subordinate interactions, was significant. Her master was no longer flirting and complaining, but rather resuming control. The animal looked away from the man standing near them and moved toward Bodkin. She stopped next to where he lounged in the chair, facing him, as he removed a long nylon leash from the front of his backpack. The leash was wrapped in a bundle around a plain leather collar, to which no tag was attached. Bodkin unraveled the two accessories.

As he reached out to place the collar on Sheba, the dog turned away and faced the man in uniform again. The apparent cop had adjusted his arms from hands-on-waist to folded across his chest, and had taken a step toward them. Bodkin verified the continued nonlethal posture of the stranger, then hooked a hand around Sheba's back. He yanked the dog toward him, lifting her front feet from the sand. After her spell of vigilance was broken, Sheba once again resumed a passive posture, and held still as Bodkin attached the collar, then the leash. He trapped the other end of the leash under his right thigh.

The man in uniform kept his eye on the dog, and walked forward to where Bodkin could see him.

"You Lee Bodkin?" the man said.

"Am I under oath?" Bodkin said.

"No, of course not," the man said. "I think you're him, though."

Bodkin just returned the man's eye contact, trying to look pleasant. Seeing what the guy knew, offering him little.

"You know a Sheriff McCabe way up there in Minnesota? In White Pine County, I guess they call it."

Bodkin waited a six-count, then said, "Who are you?"

"Grady Morton. Chicola Police Department."

"Let me ask you something, Mr. Morton."

"Sergeant."

"Sergeant Morton. Do you normally interrogate sunbathing tourists?"

"Well," said Morton, glancing at the sand again. "No. But…" He looked at Bodkin, as if for encouragement. Bodkin said nothing.

"Uhh," Morton continued. "I'm not here checking up on you or anything. Not here for any kind of enforcement…"

"You just made me leash my dog," Bodkin said.

"Oh, that. Huh huh," Morton said, the partial chuckle coming out kind of weak. "Truth be told, Mr. Bodkin…can I call you that?"

"You seem to have decided that's who I am. So why not?"

"I kind of need your help," Morton said.

Bodkin wasn't sure of the entire scenario here, but on the issue of this guy needing help, Bodkin pretty much concurred. "How so?" Bodkin said.

"We've had some trouble recently."

Bodkin waited a moment, then asked, "When, where, and what kind?"

"Two days ago. Less than a mile from here. Murder," Morton said.

"And the killer's still out there?"

"Yes."

"Looks like I timed my vacation perfectly," Bodkin said. The lieutenant looked at him, as if wondering how Bodkin could have known it was all going to happen, and then arrange to be here accordingly.

"Just kidding, sir," Bodkin said. "Sarcasm."

"Oh, got it," Morton said.

"How did you know someone named 'Lee Bodkin' was in town? Allegedly."

"Well, we pretty much run the names on all guests who check into any of the hotels here. Routinely," Morton said.

"On *all* of them?" Bodkin said.

"Yep. It's Chief Felton's idea. He's the police chief here."

"I gathered," Bodkin said. "Kind of an invasion of privacy, isn't it?"

"Depends," Morton said. "You wouldn't believe some of the creeps who come to the Florida Panhandle to get away from their responsibilities, some from their crimes. And to flee the cold. It's quiet here, and they know it. Try to reinvent themselves, false ID and the whole bit. But initially we can detect them."

"Because they often present their actual ID upon first arriving. Just haven't had the time to get set up with the phony persona yet," Bodkin said.

"Bingo," Morton said.

"Kind of a slow schedule for your department, it seems, if you find the time to do all that tourist perusal," Bodkin said.

"We're anything but slow. Being alerted to an armed felon or a nutjob in advance, before they settle in, can help keep a demanding load from becoming impossible," Morton said. "Anyway…"

"Anyway," Bodkin said.

"Your name came up as significant. It was flagged per our data drilldown. Further digging revealed a track record of your working as a freelancer for the Feds, as well as for smaller agencies. Some bounty hunting efforts; some deep woods pursuit of bad guys. Plus lots of other stuff involving a gun and a dog, it suggested."

Morton paused. Bodkin remained quiet.

"We liked what we saw, if you want the truth. As you suggested, the timing of you being here seems almost like serendipity," Morton said.

"Why? I'm just a tourist on vacation," Bodkin said.

"Uh, you're more than that, I believe. One of your past employers, a certain Sheriff McCabe who I mentioned, told us you were a definite go-to resource. A real standup guy also. It sounds like you're some kind of hero for hire," Morton said.

"I've been accused of a lot of things, but being a hero was never one of them," Bodkin said.

"Well, I'd be willing to refer to you as just that if you'd take a break from vacation to pitch in. No money has been set aside or raised for your fee, but Felton said he would look into it. As soon as you agree to sign up."

"Murder of a citizen is normally a police issue," Bodkin said. He looked away from Morton, back out toward the water.

"I wish it were that simple," Morton said. "The victims weren't assailed in town, nor on the beach."

Bodkin continued to examine the gently pulsing ocean water.

"They were attacked in the swampland. In one of our area parks. Kind of a primitive sprawl back there. Like being down south of here in the Everglades, sort of."

Bodkin didn't respond.

"Brutalized. Both of them. One was a young gal, the other a strapping, speedy football player from the local college. Both were beaten and then stabbed in the head, it seems like. Or maybe bitten, we're not sure."

Bodkin turned his face to Morton, resuming eye contact. He wanted to continue his act of indifference, but this unsure policeman now had his attention.

"Go on," Bodkin said.

"Both victims appeared to have been taken by surprise. Neither had even started to run away, evidence suggests. Seems the killer or killers got the jump on them. Not good."

"I would certainly agree there," Bodkin said.

"So, not so simple. Plus, there may be more victims than just these last two. We have some families living in our county, but not in town exactly. Out in the wetland areas, rather. In little mossy shacks, that type of thing. Kind of wild people, more or less. Huh huh," Morton said, concluding with a chuckle.

"That's how I live, in fact," Bodkin said.

"No offense meant. Huh," Morton said, following it up with a weak grin.

"So what about these rural people, Sergeant?"

"Two are missing. One dad from the Wyland family, and a teenage daughter from the Erskin family."

"For how long?" Bodkin said.

"The dad two months, the daughter almost three weeks," Morton said.

"Maybe they just up and left."

"Perhaps. The likelihood of it doesn't lean that way, though."

"Have you issued a cautionary communiqué to area residents in any way?" Bodkin asked.

"Uh, we're working on that," Morton said.

Silence drifted between them for almost a minute. Bodkin then said, "I'm sure your team will find a worthwhile direction to pursue. Or are they overworked? Cuz I must say, your approach here is a bit strange."

"Agreed. Of course, Florida is known for being strange," Morton said.

"So I heard," Bodkin said.

"Um, yeah, about that. The team, I mean."

"What?"

"The team's a little small. In fact…"

Don't tell me, thought Bodkin.

"It's been assigned to just me," Morton said.

Whoops. This Morton guy was the entire team. No wonder he was here, seeking help.

Bodkin hoped the doubt didn't show on his face. He glanced for a microsecond at Morton's beaten up, black leather uniform shoes, his low-capacity handgun and its old holster. His lack of confidence. No commando was Morton.

"Can't anyone else in your department keep you company?" Bodkin said.

"Only eight of us total. Sparing other officers from their normal duties just won't work. And this isn't even spring break season," Morton said.

From the sound of it, this dude Morton was getting a major operation dumped in his lap, to conduct alone. It would be impossible. Under normal circumstances, fully staffed police departments put more effort into enforcing traffic violations.

Not sure what to say next, Bodkin looked over at his dog. She had no opinion.

"You've chased after criminals in swamps and marshes, the information shows," Morton said.

"A little, yeah," Bodkin said. "Some action in the thick stuff, as needed."

It was actually Bodkin's specialty.

"And the data showed that you came to the rescue during the infamous New Orleans disaster awhile back. For some of the most endangered folks there. You eliminated some threats, in one way or another."

Bodkin started to grin. "Yeah, I guess that's accurate…one way or another. Nice way to put it. That hurricane mess resulted in kind of a free-for-all. But long story short, a large number of volunteers helped out in

New Orleans. My actions there just blended in with the rest of the efforts. Nothing special."

"That's not what the reports described. I wouldn't have wanted to be on the receiving end of your 'actions,' as you describe them. If even half of the stuff described in the report is true."

Bodkin let his eyes wander upwards to the sky, examining the thick clouds, white against blue. Again he didn't respond.

"Considering your capabilities, you might want to come on board. Get some more experience, make a little dough on the side," Morton said.

While considering the mission he'd just completed up north, Bodkin did an inventory on his body for a few seconds. Wrenched neck; sore left wrist, sore right ankle. Tender lower back; exhausted shoulders, general systemic fatigue. All magnified by his natural inclination toward laziness, which he hadn't been able to indulge much for the past few years. But which he planned to here and now, next to the sunny gulf. Despite all that, he was presently being asked to come off this chair on the beach, to once again fight the good fight.

"Forget about it," Bodkin said.

"What if the price was right?" Morton said.

"No dice," Bodkin said. "I'm on R and R."

It was Morton's turn to look out at the ocean, then examine the sky. After a few seconds, he looked back at Bodkin.

"Thanks for your time, and welcome. Enjoy Chicola," Morton said. He turned and shuffled off through the sand.

Bodkin waited a few moments, still gazing at the shore. His usual nudge of guilt started to poke at his soul; he worked to force it away. A familiar struggle for Bodkin. A weakness.

Victims beaten and then stabbed in the head…

If there was some kind of killer back in the density, crafty enough to slink through a humid swampland morass, skilled at ambushing, and brutal enough to kill people by stabbing them in the head…

Or maybe bitten…we're not sure.

Then this Morton guy was in big trouble. He looked like he struggled with the stealth required to just walk across the sand.

Future victims would also remain in trouble, since the cops here had issued no warning to area residents yet. Unreal. They were being kept in the dark. The citizens would thus continue to be vulnerable to a surprise attack…just as the now dead ones apparently were.

Bodkin and his partner had worked situations like this before. He knew the bodies could really stack up if a serial killer was on a frenzy. Especially if nobody knew there was one out there; especially if they were allowed by the authorities to be sitting ducks.

Bodkin also knew he himself could in fact help matters here. It was the kind of situation he was designed for.

One of the two voices inside Bodkin was telling him that. From the logical side of his brain. The voice from the other side, the side seeking rest, pleasure, food…sun…sleep…countered the thought.

I'm on R and R, it said.

"Let me know when he's out of sight, girl," Bodkin said to Sheba. The dog watched calmly in the direction that Morton had walked, and 12 seconds later, nudged Bodkin's hand with her nose. Bodkin reached up to the snap on the leash, unhooked it, then unfastened the collar. He dropped both to the sand, stroked his dog's head a few times, then leaned back again in the plastic lounge chair. He flipped his Costa Del Mars back on.

"Go lie down or wander around a little. Find some sand crabs or something," Bodkin said to her.

Then he closed his eyes, and felt the sun's warm glow envelope him.

3

The creature surveyed the potential prey. It decided it had to take them. Just had to.

It was spurred on by the frantic movement of the humans – the jumping, twisting, and shouting. The glee. Spurred on by those things, and also enraged.

The creature could never fully grasp the intricacies of glee and happiness, but it knew the emotions when it saw them. And hated the owners of those feelings, the purveyors of those wonderful expressions. The creature itself only experienced similar feelings during a kill, as well as right afterward. Then the feelings would vanish, replaced by edginess, irritation, and aggression.

Today the sounds had been easy to detect from deep in the swampland, as the beings that emitted them were essentially screeching and yelling. The presence of its intended quarry, and consequently the associated sounds, only occurred at exact times of the day. And this activity occurred most days, but not all. The creature had no way to catalogue exactly when the arrival and departure happened, other than noting that it happened just after sunrise and a few hours before dark.

It had in fact heard the ruckus starting again this morning. And when it did, the creature hustled through the swampy thickness to again engage in its surveillance. Its urges were pushing the creature to a decision in this matter: there had been enough wondering, yearning, and wanting. The creature was finally going to act on this temptation. Soon.

But the burly beast had to be careful. Of danger and detection this simple-thinking killer was fully aware. To leave concealment, to exit the musty, wet swamp tangles, was to expose itself. Make itself vulnerable.

To attention. To identification. To alarm. To danger, such as human beings with their thunder makers.

It didn't understand the workings of a gun, but knew what constituted one. What a gun looked like, more or less. And that giving a human the chance to use said gun could mean its own death. Yes, leaving cover was a great risk to take.

But with the quarry in question, and the sure kills they presented, wasn't the risk worth it? Wasn't the excitement, and the vengeance, worth it?

No. No. No, the creature's instincts sounded off. Not worth risking life and limb, it felt, in a vague sense. But when reminding itself of the joy it would feel with the execution of the victims…and the nutrient solution it could obtain from them, from inside their skulls…the other voice inside voted otherwise.

The voice of passion. Of appetite.

Yes. Yes. Yes.

It would have them, it would take them.

Yes.

Their killings were not an absolute necessity for the creature's survival, and they were not executions of precision. Rather, they were an outpouring of rage. The creature didn't have any idea why it often felt such acute anger. The answer lay in its ancestry, and the result of a splicing of genetics, but those details were beyond the brute's grasp. Regardless, explosively committing the two murders diffused its hostility somewhat. Its rage cycled instead of remaining a constant, allowing the creature to retain just enough caution and elusiveness to avoid detection. To avoid capture.

And the blood and fluids the thing had consumed from inside the skulls were merely a fringe benefit. The violent creature was actually a true omnivore. It preferred to eat the copious plant matter the swampland provided: mulberries, pond apples, hickory nuts, and coco plums. These were sometimes mixed in with an occasional frog, snake, or salamander, or maybe an entire nest of carpenter ants. But very rarely was the food from plants and trees coupled with meat and blood from larger prey. That is, unless the creature was denied for a long period of time of its main adversary, and its favorite prey of all.

Human beings.

Then it tended to indulge fully, with the creature afterward left glowing from some of the victims' brain matter along with the satisfaction of the kill.

Time now to watch and learn. Recognize habits, memorize routines. From a human perspective, the creature may have been a simpleton. A brute. But one thing it did better than most predators. Than most humans, for that matter. In regard to hunting prey, it possessed a distinct advantage over most other carnivores. Over virtually all reptiles, as well as over most mammals. The advantage was one gained from observing and learning the activity of its quarry.

It was such a simple – but important – advantage: after observing the behaviors of its prey, it *remembered*. Since it had the capacity to remember, it could plan accordingly. To the detriment of many of its chosen victims.

As the creature gazed over the expanse of the creek, toward the prey, it heard the swishing of countless tiny minnows in the water below. Following the tiny silver shapes were larger fish, which twirled and swirled in the shallow creek as they consumed the minnows. Another predator-prey instance. In other circumstances, the creature would have appreciated the relationship, and would have taken the time to observe the action. All while it worked out a plan to capture a few of the larger fish, to take as its own to feast upon.

But not now. With the prey on the land across the creek darting and jumping and playing, the creature couldn't have cared less about the little fish below. Neither the tiny ones nor the larger ones that ate them.

It continued to look across the creek at the prey items on land. As often happened, the targeted prey became partially obscured by the moving shelter, as it rumbled and crawled past their location. The massive shelter that brought them here each time, and that later came to meet them and carry them off. It was always the same gigantic bulk, noisy and smelly. And yellow. The small prey beings would run out from inside of it when they arrived, often chirping with excitement. They'd also do the same later in the day as they ran back into the hulking container. The shelter would then grind and cough, and move its strange round legs in order to go into motion. Taking them away, leaving the creature there, alone and watching. And wanting.

The shelter moved away in similar fashion now, but as usual, left without the quarry. It traveled to the left of the scene, and the creature once again could see the prey. Its future victims. Ones it had already claimed as its own. The creature watched as the prey ran away to their lair, where they would stay for a long period, into the afternoon, until the yellow moving shelter came back to whisk them away again.

The creature watched them for another few seconds. Then, once all of the children had run inside of the single story building, the creature looked away, trembling with excitement, and slunk into the brush. All the while treasuring the chance to once again view the kids before they ran into Chicola Elementary.

4

"Yep, they come up right into the creek. Easy pickins."

"How do I find the creek?" asked Lee Bodkin.

"Oh, it runs right through town there," said the proprietor of the Knick Knack Shack. He'd introduced himself to Bodkin as Walton.

Bodkin would soon learn that he should have stayed in the plastic chaise lounge, soaking up sun. But as in most cases when he unwittingly flung himself into a perilous mess, it was due to restlessness. Eagerness. Anticipation of possibilities.

Now, it was the possibility of adventure. Of conquest. And of food.

The first two factors mattered, but it was the food thing that pretty much pushed Bodkin over the edge. As per usual. After a glorious 23-minute nap on the beach, he awoke, stared at the sand and water for a few minutes, then popped up to his feet. With thoughts of buttered fish fillets in his mind, he went down along the shore toward town, to find answers.

Bodkin only had to wander for a mere seven minutes, still staying on the beach, until he happened upon the Knick Knack Shack. It wasn't hard to locate. Very few other vendors existed in the area, and save for the Knick Knack Shack, exactly zero were open for business. More would be once the spring break crowds arrived, but not now. The Knick Knack Shack was a simple hut selling most any item beachgoers might want.

The shack captured the whole laid back Florida sand-and-surf thing; it even had its own genuine beach bum running the show.

"Yep, from Barrier Creek you should be able to pull out a nice mess of sea trout," Walton said, leaning out from the hut's serving window. He gave Bodkin an assured glance, as if delivering very good news. Then Walton looked down at his bag of trail mix, where the peanuts, raisins, and walnuts were getting in the way of the M&Ms. He pushed aside a couple of nuts and secured one of the elusive candy orbs, an orange one, triumphantly crunching it up.

Here was Bodkin taking advice – *fishing* advice of all things – from a dude who possibly had never ventured into the world of swamp tangles and rugged wild things. Well, at least he didn't look the part. With age comes wisdom, perhaps? You could never tell. The guy appeared to be a decade older or so than Bodkin himself, but not really any wiser. Make that much less wiser, Bodkin sensed. With his worn-out organic cotton button down, mostly unbuttoned and uneven across his shoulders, and his sun-kissed face and long brown and silver hair arranged in partial Rastafarian dreadlock styling, this Walton guy was striving for an image. He may have been achieving whatever that image was supposed to be, but certainly not that of an outdoorsman.

Nevertheless, Bodkin played the part of the attentive student/tourist, awaiting advice. Hey, why not? In this case the advice was free.

"Sounds cool. What approach do you recommend? With tackle, lures, and all," Bodkin said.

"Live bait will work for the critters, but you don't need it. It's more trouble to carry and keep the bait alive than it's worth," Walton said.

"OK," Bodkin said.

"Keep the line narrow. Around 4-pound test at the most. Even better is 2-pound. Fluorocarbon line is a better choice than monofilament, since it's essentially invisible. Follow?"

"Yep."

"Like trout anywhere, they're vulnerable to spinners. Willow leaf blades are best, if you have any," Walton said.

"I do." Maybe Walton wasn't so clueless after all.

"Great. But nothing over size 1, maybe even stick with size 0. Gotta keep the bait small, because the pinfish minnows they hammer are quite diminutive."

Diminutive. Nice. Walton was possibly well-read. Bodkin was liking this guy better by the moment.

"But a spinner is a secondary lure for the sea trout. The pinfish swim with more of a wave motion, not a jitter, you could say. So ideally, you want to use a marabou jig. Know what that is?" Walton asked.

"Yes. With the soft feathers." Well-read and fish-savvy. Bodkin was silently starting to eat his unspoken words about the sundry shack owner.

"Right. The motion of the feathers imitate an exhausted pinfish minnow. The sea trout rise to inhale the tired ones first," Walton said.

"How considerate of them," Bodkin said.

"Nature is brutal," Walton said.

"Kind of like our species," Bodkin said.

"All species of everything, if you examine things deeply enough. Anyway, once again, no line over 4-pound test. The sea trout don't like to see line swimming around. It spooks them," Walton said. He located another M&M, a green one this time, and dispatched it without mercy.

Maybe Bodkin didn't know it all, and maybe regarding the subject of resident fish, Mr. Walton here did. After all, he was from the area, and despite Bodkin writing him off initially, the guy probably dabbled in the sea trout harvest himself. Truthfully, there were characters with similar disheveled personas who actually made a living as fishing guides in saltwater and bayou locales; guys who were better fishermen than Bodkin would ever dream of being. Bodkin should have known better than to judge by first impressions.

The harvest of spotted sea trout had been on Bodkin's mind for months. It started with the knowledge that the Florida Panhandle experienced a spotted sea trout feeding frenzy every year around late November. That figured into his being here at this time of the year; if the trout run was at the end of December, that month would have been his targeted time frame. Middle of January? Then Bodkin's preference would have adjusted accordingly. Hungry fish trumped vacationing convenience.

So did his chosen profession. Many a vacation plan in the past had been foiled by Bodkin's assignments, with their unpredictability. Conversely, sometimes Lady Luck smiles down: clearing the assignments on his plate this time worked out perfectly for a vacation at the peak of the trout frenzy. Now Bodkin would soon capitalize.

But in moderation. Good old Walton here was steering him in the right direction. Encouraging him and enabling him to go out and score on a heap of fish; or as Walton said, a "mess" of them.

Which Bodkin wouldn't do. Walton didn't need to know it, but Bodkin had a specific harvest goal: two total fish. Two nice fat ones; the rest he'd unhook and release, let them swim to fight again. The unlucky ones he secured would be filleted at creekside, and the meat slabs brought back to the hotel, where the kitchenette awaited. The first fish morsels would be fried in onions, butter, and curry for Bodkin; the second batch would be simply steamed in water, and dropped into Sheba's dish. Half of each fish devoured the first day, the second half of the meat the next. Fresh from the ocean, plucked from the creek, then savored by the human predator and his dog. Bodkin almost smiled thinking about it.

With thoughts of those fleshy fish in his mind, Bodkin finished up the tutorial with Walton. Then Walton switched gears.

"Be careful out there, Lee Roy."

"Lee."

"Oh, yeah. Lee. The reason I say be careful…well…" Walton's voiced drifted off, as if thinking the better of continuing.

"I heard some people got killed," Bodkin said. "That what you're talking about?"

"Yep. A popular college football player and a lady friend of his."

"I heard the same. Not sure what that has to do with me, though."

"Well, the creek you're gonna be fishing goes into a pretty brushy area. Big cypress trees, palmetto thickets. Density, you know," Walton said.

"I know density well," Bodkin said. "So?"

Walton fiddled with his trail mix, settling this time for an almond.

"Details?" Bodkin said. "Supposed serial killer?"

Walton simply chewed, stalling.

"Hey, friend, you brought it up," Bodkin continued. Walton remained quiet. "Well, thanks for the fishing tips, in any case. I'll be off," Bodkin said.

"Uh, well, wait," Walton said. "Like we just covered, killings have occurred. Sadly. But you know, man, this violence is a new type of event in the area. We have always had the presence of homicide in the region, of course. Pretty much shootings and knifings, sometimes clubbings and stompings. Usually accompanied by alcohol. But some new factor might be around now. The killings have been done back in the thick greenery, and the victims have been basically beaten to death."

Bodkin maintained eye contact, and remained quiet.

"Beaten to death, but with teeth marks left in them," Walton said. Teeth marks. That matched up with what Sergeant Morton had claimed. "Certain people outside of town, the marsh dwellers you might call them, are really intimate with the swamp. With the types of beasts there, and the type of transient weirdos who may pass through. I trust what they say about this new threat; these are folks I've known my whole life."

"What do they say?" Bodkin said.

"Some people here think we have a Bigfoot on our hands."

"Huh?"

"A Bigfoot. You know, like the legendary Sasquatch."

Ooo-kay.

"Is that a recurring problem in these parts?" Bodkin asked. He should have known; this guy was typical of a recreational drug enthusiast. Maybe magic mushrooms? The hallucinogens could be doing the talking now.

"Don't be glib, partner," Walton said. "This is a serious issue we face. Two victims have been found dead, but four more of our neighbors are missing."

"Four?" Bodkin recalled that Morton had said two. In spite of himself, he was smiling a little, stimulated by the thoughts of how quickly this was becoming ludicrous. And the tales were growing taller. Walton caught the smile.

"Yes. And don't worry, I can count that high. I know that you might not assume so, being a Northern sophisticate and all," Walton said. "I can tell this amuses you."

"Let's talk about the Sasquatch theory, Walton," Bodkin said, wiping his face clean of the smile. It still flirted inside of him, however. "You were trying to warn me, I recall."

"Yes, of course. So, looks like four other people or so have been attacked, in addition to the football player and his girl pal. The last two had their brutalized bodies found; the others, that's anyone's guess. Not everything that happens in the marshland gets reported to the authorities, trust me. Regarding the others, here's what we know. Awhile back, one man out there in the marsh heard a cry for help near his home. He went out to see what was going on. He and his daughter both. And they…"

Walton paused.

"You're not a cop are you?"

"Far from it," Bodkin said.

"Then some kind of ex-soldier or something, I think," Walton said.

"Just a Northern sophisticate on vacation," Bodkin said.

Walton appraised Bodkin, then went on. "I just had a hunch, that's all. Your buzzed hair and that thick shoulder look suggested it. My mistake. All right, so this guy, name of Hubert Tollig…well, the dude swears he saw it up close. Some kind of dark animal thing, could lean forward and move on all fours, but also stand and run upright."

Bodkin figured the story was being embellished, or even made up. He didn't make a comment to Walton as such; instead, he thought about what he'd just heard.

Could stand and run upright. Big deal. That would be what any human assailant would be doing if victims were to be captured. And 'dark thing'? Any old outfit of black, dark grey, and navy blue could make it so.

But what about this 'moving on all fours' business? Bodkin hoped that part was just added on for dramatic effect. Really hoped it.

"Hubert Tollig is an aging, toothless guy, drinks a lot. A lot of people don't believe him – about anything – when he comes into town. So this time old Hubert did them one better." Walton looked at Bodkin, waiting for him to ask how.

"How?" Bodkin asked.

"He took two snapshots of it. See, they give free cell phones to the poorest folks in the county here…and…"

"Did you see either photo?" Bodkin said.

"Yep. Both," Walton said.

He looked at Bodkin, as if his point had been proven. Bodkin looked back, waiting.

"A couple of days after that event, Tollig had a few beers at the main pub in town, The Tentacle," Walton said. "He's trying to sell the photos to a TV station, he told a few of us. He'll sell to any station that'll take them. Contacted places in Miami, Atlanta, Charlotte, Jacksonville, plus some other joints. Still waiting on an answer from one of them."

"Looking for that pay day," Bodkin said.

"Oh yeah. Hopes to make a killing, for the first time in his life. That's when he showed the pics to a few of us. The shots are still on his phone. His only copies of the pics I bet."

"Plenty of faith in the digital universe," Bodkin said.

"Yeah, for sure. Anyway, he said he's keeping it quiet, as he believes the police chief here would seize the phone and its contents as evidence. And I think the chief would. The police chief here is kind of a totalitarian type."

"With what I hear of spring break melees, not sure I blame him. Do you yourself believe it's true? That the photos were genuine?" Bodkin asked.

"Sure do. They were just too imperfect to be altered shots," Walton said. "If a person was to Photoshop something like that, it would have a more precise look, I'd think. These shots on his phone only show part of a dark figure in the brush, like a lowered head and its shoulders. The thing looks like it's lunging in the direction of the person taking the pictures. The second picture is closer than the first. Scary, I must say. But I'm no authority, one way or another. I'm a shack owner selling odds and ends, and don't want to be much else."

"Why only two pics?" Bodkin said. "If I was taking shots I thought I could make money from, I'd snap a bunch of them. Get 'em while the getting's good."

"That your policy?" Walton said.

"Sure. You ought to see me in the grocery store when they put out free samples. So, why just two pics?"

"Because the dark thing rushed him. He and his daughter. That's what he told me at the bar, anyway. He said they managed to get back inside his house and hide," Walton said. "If his daughter ran away, believe me, something frightening was coming. She's late thirties, strong, irreverent. Kind of a bar brawler…"

"Not exactly the belle of the ball, huh?" Bodkin said.

"No, definitely not. Can take a lot of the guys on in the hard-drinking crowd. If she was scared, it means something."

"I've seen the type. So why won't this Tollig individual simply share copies of the pics with the cops here, then go on trying to get a station to buy them as well?" Bodkin asked.

"Like I said, he thinks the police here would lay claim to the photos exclusively," Walton said. "That's why I asked if you were a cop or not. The chief here might try to make a big deal out of it if he learns Tollig has pictures of what could be the attacker. And that Tollig was withholding those pictures. Course, I don't see what Tollig could be charged with for simply keeping what's his."

Obstruction of justice, maybe?

"Have you folks considered that it was just a black bear? Or a hog? I know you have scads of both here," Bodkin said.

"Ha," Walton said. "That old man, Hubert…sure you're not with the cops?"

Bodkin just looked back, bored. Walton inserted a red M&M into his mouth, crushed it, then continued.

"Well, Tollig over the years has hunted down and eaten dozens of both animals. Likes bear meat, will eat hog steaks when he can get them. So he knows the difference. Part of how he's kept fed all these years," Walton said. "He does it off the record, so to speak."

"Gotta make ends meet," Bodkin said. "So you've concluded that if it's not a big pig or a bear, it must be a Sasquatch."

"I do think the arrival of one of those Bigfoot beasts makes sense. Two reasons."

"Let's hear 'em," Bodkin said. He'd humor this guy, considering the free fishing advice and all.

"OK, here's the first reason why," Walton said. "With all of Tollig's calling around, word got out. I mean, how could it not? And one of the parties the news reached was some institute out west. They study and document paranormal stuff, super beings, weird animals, extraterrestrials, you know."

"So naturally Sasquatch encounters and sightings," Bodkin said.

"Naturally," Walton said. "The people at this institute wanted to talk to anyone in authority here to find out more. To find out which big wigs in Chicola might have inside info."

"But what does their contacting your town leaders prove?" Bodkin asked.

Walton shrugged. "I figure, if the folks at that institute took notice, calling the city manager and police chief, then why, there might be something to this. It might actually be a Sasquatch sneaking around. The institute crew may know how to track migrations or movements, or whatever Bigfoot specimens do."

"Yes, they may," Bodkin said. "What else?"

"One or more of the mysterious beasts traveling into the region would make sense, based on the fact that Mississippi and Louisiana seem to have very few reports of Sasquatch sightings over the last several years," Walton said. "They used to have many. So, if there's some kind of a migration, why not over here?"

It was Bodkin's turn to shrug.

"That second bit of logic comes from my contacts in town," Walton said.

"Your cronies at The Tentacle?" Bodkin said.

"Yep."

"Enthusiasts, apparently."

"Very much so," Walton said. "For that type of thing, plus anything dealing with the swamp or the sea really. That's our life in these parts, after all."

"Excellent. Thanks for the warning; I'm much better informed now, and feel safer," Bodkin said. He smiled a genuine smile at Walton, doing the best to conceal any laughter that struggled to rise up. "Is that trail mix something you sell here?"

"Sure is. Just unloading a new batch. Like a few packs?" Walton said.

"Just one. All the bags have M&Ms, I hope."

"Certainly do. Wouldn't have any other composition," Walton said. Bodkin figured Walton would feel that way.

Walton reached into a cardboard box on a shelf behind him, scooped out a bag and handed it to Bodkin.

"Just three dollars," Walton said with pride.

Bodkin handed him a five, then dropped the change into the Knick Knack Shack's tip canister.

"So, anyway…Lee is it?" Walton said.

Walton would never make it as a politician.

"That's right. Lee," Bodkin said. Smiling again, amused, but Walton took it as simple congeniality.

"When you go after the trout, besides watching your back, make sure that you don't go heavy with line or lures," Walton said. "Because, the little minnows the trout eat are, you know…"

"Diminutive," Bodkin suggested.

"Exactly. Couldn't have said it better myself."

"One last question regarding fishing," Bodkin said.

"Sure."

"How do I know which one is Barrier Creek?"

"Well, to drive there from the center of town, just take Palm Parkway to 9th Avenue, then a left onto Spinnaker. Follow that until you see the creek," Walton said.

"Hmm," Bodkin said. "The water eventually drains into the gulf, right?"

"Of course."

'Can't I get there from the beach in that case?"

"Sure you could," Walton said. "You have 4-wheel drive?"

"Yeah, but I'd rather just hike over," Bodkin said.

"You sure?" Walton said. "Must be over a half-mile."

"I think I'll manage," Bodkin said. He, along with Sheba and his partner Gladdis, had often tracked fugitives for miles, and for days. "But there are a few creeks along the shore. And you said that only one of them, Barrier Creek, has the trout navigating up it."

"Yep."

"So, from the beach, how do I know which stream is the correct one?"

"I think it's the fourth or fifth one you'll come across from here," Walton said. "But there's only one way to tell for sure."

"Which is?"

"When you're at the correct creek and you look upstream, you can see the top of a building through the trees. You're at the right creek if you spot the building. It's the creek running right past the grade school, Chicola Elementary."

5

Terrence Powell couldn't believe the luck. The awesome luck.

He'd scored a major hit on the institute's radar; plus, the category he'd be investigating was his favorite. And on top of it all, the new find would allow him to travel to a tropical climate.

And in late November, no less. Perfect excuse to escape the Western Wyoming winter for a little while.

As Associate Director of the Unidentified Species Unit at the Enlighten Institute, Powell was the primary resource for identifying and tracking down promising and mysterious leads. In some cases, these morsels of evidence resulted in actual encounters with mysterious beings. In more instances, the hunches and clues led to dead ends. You could never know for sure, so you had to check out any and all leads with high potential.

This could include leads on all sorts of life forms, specifically those bizarre and off the beaten path: strange spiritual forces, mutant hybrids, and creatures possibly from other planets.

And, yes, anything pointing to evidence of Sasquatch. That elusive species had frustrated and excited his organization for years…since the group's inception, really. Clues of Sasquatch had been found in abundance, with sightings and photos almost certainly verifying a Sasquatch presence in so many locales in North America.

Nobody had ever come in close contact with a Sasquatch yet, and certainly no one had ever communicated with one of them. Yet, the Sasquatch possibilities formed a major part of the Enlighten Institute's backbone, one of their prominent reasons for being.

Situated in Jackson Hole, Wyoming, the institute had immediate access to Yellowstone National Park and the rest of the Rocky Mountain range. Naturally, that meant access to all the denizens that lurked within those mountains…and indeed some very strange ones were found there occasionally. Very strange in fact, which fit Powell's interests and talents perfectly. And they now had the technology to expand those interests and related findings into the stratosphere.

With some of the Enlighten Institute's nifty electronic technological devices, purchased through massive corporate endowments, Powell had initiated an alert over the national radio airwaves. It was the most efficient and effective system a researcher of alternative life forms could imagine.

The radio message interceptor device used to issue the alert was no bigger than a small laptop. Yet with it he could, as they say, set it and forget it, while it scoped out thousands of communication threads per week. If key words with which the radio monitor was programmed to go off were mentioned, he'd be notified by receiving a text message and an e-mail. Then on the device itself, the screen on his alert mechanism would show the radio station and its location.

From that point, it was up to Powell or one of his staff to make calls and find out details. Assertive questioning of the people they called was the norm, and aggressive interrogation was used if needed. Authorities didn't like dealing with information that they didn't want to assume responsibility for…or that they thought they could keep secret and profit from. Had to yank it out of them sometimes, a routine process for Terrence Powell.

Just mention the institute's connection with the U.S. Fish and Wildlife Service, federal powers, blah blah blah, and the other group often cooperated. The claims Powell would make were only half truths, but the approach was generally effective.

Once information was secured, he and his team would evaluate it. If the details looked significant, as in a unique and strange life source of any kind – or much better, one of their sought-after living marvel types – that locale just might get a visit from Powell's team.

The alert earlier today signaled evidence of a sighting of Powell's primary research interest: *Sasquatch.*

Magnificent. A Sasquatch beast promised to be a discovery, a prize, without peer. A true, living marvel.

And this time, Powell would be traveling there alone. Couldn't have a team sharing credit with him on a Sasquatch encounter. Not one of his colleagues, and not even a subordinate. Especially regarding what he was determined to pioneer eventually; hopefully on this particular case it would finally happen. It would be groundbreaking if so. A first.

Powell would most likely have the track in the wilderness all to himself. The Florida Panhandle area had very little drive or interest to uncover Sasquatch occurrences. Little was ever reported there regarding sightings or suspicions. The recent intercepted messages, and there were several, revealed a backwoods type of man, obviously a nonintellectual., trying his best to peddle some photos to a large number of news stations in the Southeast. He said the images were of what he swore was a Sasquatch. The institute had captured such messages in the past, ones that turned out to be nothing.

But this time, with their snooping and hacking devices, Powell and his team also got possession of an e-mail the hayseed Florida man had shot off to a station in

Charleston. That changed everything. The object moving toward the camera in the high-action pic had a realism to it that shocked Powell. Doubtful that the photo was a fraud. Powell knew the difference.

Imagine. A massive event, a Sasquatch encounter, and one documented on film at that, pulled off not by a seasoned researcher, but instead by just some clueless redneck from the sticks. Once down in Florida, Powell would contact that guy, get as much information as possible, and take it from there. Heck, he could probably take over the rights to those photos by offering the dude $100 or so. Powell would see how low the guy would go.

Time now to organize, and prepare to roll out.

In a few hours, Powell would head out from Jackson Hole, on a puddle jumper to Pocatello, Idaho. Then he'd switch over onto a standard plane from there bound for Tallahassee, Florida. Next secure a rental car and partake in a bit of open road relaxation as he headed to the obscure town called Chicola.

Here was the outing where Powell would finally establish direct communication with a Sasquatch. He had confidence that this would be it, the special meeting and interaction of two unique species.

He'd initially befriend it. Then Powell would have an unprecedented conversation with Bigfoot, and he would then forever be famous in his circle of colleagues. He'd be the one to first speak to Sasquatch. Terrence Powell was certain of it.

6

Irwin Kagel couldn't believe the luck. The horrible luck.

How could such a grand endeavor, with such noble intentions, go astray? Not just astray, but with almost opposite results of what was envisioned?

Man plans, God laughs. Wasn't that how the saying went? If God was laughing about this situation, he was the only one. Irwin Kagel sure wasn't. And neither was the town of Chicola.

As an indirect result of Kagel's efforts, people were now dead, probably more of them than the community realized. Many of the peasants in the area recently had family members and friends go missing, and were distraught over their disappearances. Wondering where on earth their kin were, and what could have happened. Kagel was beyond wondering. He pretty much knew.

He raised the shot glass of rum to his lips. A disciplined man, Kagel hated to drink to excess. But he had to snap this numbness, this immobilized feeling. He sipped the last few drops, then grabbed the bottle from the table and splashed a little more rum into the tiny glass.

What a setting in which to imbibe in this sort of drink, the elixir of revelers and pirates. Drinking it in a sanitized, spotless laboratory. Empty of any human presence, other than his own. An unlikely place to be sipping rum, all by himself.

Until recently, he'd partnered with another science worker in his endeavors, who along with Kagel recorded data, helped make progress on cures, tried new things to make breakthroughs. The world rarely appreciated biological discoveries, as it didn't understand them. But it sure needed them. The world needed Kagel's ingenuity. In turn, Kagel needed help to succeed, but suddenly had none.

Now, his only research assistant, who had doubled as his only close friend, was gone as well. Gone just like the young football jock and his love interest, that helpless young lady, recently killed in the park. Damn it all to hell.

Kagel had feelings of guilt, confusion, and despair. He hadn't actually taken part in the killings. Hadn't caused them, not directly. And the heinous problems his project tried to solve were of the utmost importance. An entire species' survival might depend on it.

Kagel hadn't taken part in the killings, but he'd sure set the stage. The force of nature had been unleashed, so to speak…and the killings soon started. Big surprise. Once it was unleashed, what else could have happened?

He'd set the stage, yes, although accidentally; now he'd have to fix it.

The frustration, the horror, was starting to eat Irwin Kagel up inside. Melting his innards, it felt like. He sipped another portion of the rum, feeling the burn as it went down. Yeah, that ought to help. Who needs internal organs?

Regarding the threat: should he sound the alarm? Tell the cops? Warn the community? He couldn't. Kagel knew he should, but he just couldn't. This lab, the entire compound, would be shut down in mere minutes. His research and advancements, his contributions and plans of action, all would cease. Forever.

Besides, more people might end up dead if he reported what he knew. A cop or two minimum, as they stumbled ahead to solve the problem. And probably some raccoon or opossum hunter the cops might hire for tracking, with a couple of beagles or coon hounds following the scent. Following it right to their death.

Of course, the scent trail was one of the keys. What was amongst these people now was no match for hunting dogs. They'd have no way to conceive of what the threat was setting them up for.

Conversely, Kagel had another resource for the scent trail pursuit. His name was Ragnor. The key defense factor in this dilemma, a factor who could follow a scent trail as well as a blood hound…but unlike a clueless dog, Ragnor knew the likely places the killer would travel. Ragnor was the best resource in the world, really, for what the people here faced.

But Kagel wasn't willing to go that far, not yet. At this point, that resource was now virtually his only companion, and was just too valuable to him. And too innocent. He couldn't put such a wonderful and precious being like Ragnor at risk, unless no other choice remained.

But that aside, Kagel had to keep in mind a new glimmer of hope. He'd just encountered it earlier today. At the diner downtown, he'd been sitting there, consuming coffee with two slices of bacon and an English muffin, the muffin smeared with apple jelly – his usual. Boring, he knew. Like him.

If you didn't believe it, you only had to ask the last 30 women he'd been interested in during his 61 years. But in any case, the lukewarm image he maintained helped Kagel to blend in, to escape notice. That image and its near invisibility had benefited him many times: in his early career years in Pittsburgh, then the Caribbean, then his most wonderful time assisting with the struggle in the Dark Continent. And it helped him again, just today. Like before, he could blend in, become the fly on the wall, listen and learn.

The blowhard police Chief, Ernest Felton, had been at the diner with another cop and one of the town selectmen. They all nodded to Kagel, saying "Morning, Dr. Kagel," or something similar, then they looked away and forgot about him. Kagel then concentrated on his plate, pretending to be deep in thought. And he listened.

He heard the expected things, about challenges in gearing up for spring break, lack of local jobs, hot weather coming just four months from now. What was new? It was Florida after all. But then…

This trio of proletariats – the police chief, his lackey, and the smarmy selectman – mentioned something about a special operative or similar arriving in town. Kagel's focus was at first increased, then it became white hot, staring at a collection of crumbs from the muffin as he listened. Bounty hunter, shooter, tracker…then a name.

Brocklin? Bomlin? Then the street cop, louder than the others, stated it more clearly.

Bodkin.

It was pretty much all Kagel needed. Shouldn't be hard to determine the spelling, from the sound of it. Then the first name was repeated: *Lee.*

Got it. Was it divine intervention? Was this character here on purpose? It didn't matter. The coincidence might be the break Kagel needed; the break his research compound required to stay afloat. The safety of people, in the mortal sense, was on the line in the Chicola area, no less. He cared about both his lab staying open and the lives of people in the community, although he wasn't sure which he'd protect first.

If things were as they appeared, this just might work. All Kagel needed was someone who would make the decisive finishing touch, like anyone who knew how to shoot back at adversaries could. His companion, Ragnor, with the special ability to track by scent, could get them there…in position. And any unapologetic killer with a gun, like a soldier, hitman, or commando, could finish it. If Kagel decided to go that far, then all would be good. He didn't like the thought of the menace, the killer creature, being wiped out, but it had to be done. At this point, it would be the only solution to stop the murders.

Bodkin. A word used by the Old English for *dagger.* Hot damn. All the research into the guy, this gun for hire, was routine. Easy to acquire. And to say the least, it was fascinating. Kagel had printed out a bunch of pages to read regarding the Bodkin fellow. The pile was next to where Kagel sat at the lab table; he picked up the printouts and started glancing through them once again.

Kagel didn't just Google people like the common person did. Due to his past efforts helping the EPA and the State Department with his research, he had special federal government clearance. On all sorts of information. As a matter of fact, on top of other privileges, he had login access to the United States Marshalls Service and FBI databases. Tons of law enforcement info at his fingertips there. Conveniently, the State Department folks forgot to revoke his privileges once his projects there were done. Kagel wasn't sure if they did this as a gesture of thanks or not, so he kept his mouth shut. And kept using that special access quite often.

So here were a few things Kagel discovered about this newly arrived man:

Lethal. No police experience. No military service. Weapons maker…but just some archery equipment, no guns or bombs or anything. That bow and arrow crafting stuff being his primary business, it turned out. Longbows mainly, kind of like medieval soldiers had used, as well as primitive peoples in earlier times. Kagel didn't imagine much money in that business, but you never know.

Of note: as a deer hunter, Bodkin took down the animals with the same primitive bows he made. The bows weren't for show.

Trained in wilderness survival and guerilla warfare. Hmm? Kagel assumed at one of those private mercenary-type camps. That was kind of creepy. On the other hand, that could be a good thing, if he was on your side…especially in a situation like Chicola's current one.

Poor, or bordering on it. No big government budget backing him up. The classic freelancer. Accomplished wrestler in his previous life, during college and immediately thereafter. Spent years on the mat working his way up to a world-level ranking on the international scene. No wonder he was poor. Should have considered football or baseball.

Expert at hand-to-hand combat. That was pretty logical with the wrestling stuff. Used simple weapons: a shotgun mainly, sometimes a revolver as backup, in rare cases a modern semiautomatic pistol. But more often, his own hands served as backup.

Additionally, this Bodkin character worked with a female partner. They'd built up a substantial resume of search-and-rescue efforts. So they displayed an altruistic side, which was usually a good thing. Search-and-rescue almost seemed to be their specialty at times, when not tied up in much more violent endeavors.

In other cases, they worked as hired muscle. Bodyguards, more or less. But leaning more toward guardians who watched from a distance. To run interference, maybe operate as snipers. Wait in the concealment where assassins were expected to approach from, then intercept them in advance. The described bodyguard detail was some of what they did, but just a small part. Kagel continued shuffling through the sheets of the federal reports, reading further.

Above all, Lee Bodkin and his partner were manhunters. Licensed bounty hunters, actually. Kind of U.S. Marshal types, so no surprise there that they contracted out to the Marshals' service.

This woman, Kagel couldn't remember the name, Gretchen Morose or something. She was said to be a competitive biathlete, on top of her high action chases after crooks for money. That should take care of the cardio requirements, without a doubt. It of course would help with shooting a rifle while on the hunt, as biathletes were required to be bullseye shooters, and do it under duress.

She was also described as a wilderness survival expert. An instructor of said skills, as a matter of fact.

While on assignment, Bodkin and his partner were classified as "expendable assets," which Kagel imagined they both realized and accepted. Par for the course in freelance soldier-style work. Ironically, operatives who didn't mind being expendable were in great demand by the government, and in turn were eager to sign up. Kagel didn't get it.

One item Kagel took notice of, resulting in some of his current glee: their activities weren't much in terms of concrete jungle stakeouts and car chases. Instead, projects were commenced more commonly outside of cities and immersed in nature. The two of them were deep cover pursuit specialists: swamp, forest, jungle. Not many could do that. Kagel could almost see the buffoon cops in town here trying it. They'd probably let the suspects run free, knock off early for a beer and a club sandwich. The main team, that is. The rest of them would then assign Officer Morton, that poor awkward guy on the local force, to do it alone. The usual procedure, as far as Kagel could tell.

Back to Bodkin and his partner. While perusing the printouts, a concern had popped up: they used an attack dog. The dog was a tracker, and the two people it ran for cooperated with it as a trio. For detection, distraction, and confusion of the fugitives. Sometimes for violent apprehension as well.

One info bit, in a file from the Foreign Protection Bureau, noted the dog was partly wolf. That caught Kagel's attention. How would that work with Ragnor? If this Bodkin guy was to sign on with Kagel, it either would be without said wolf-dog, or the thing would have to stay under close control from its owner. If it displayed an attitude toward Ragnor, or heaven forbid snapped at him, Ragnor would smash the dog like a bug. Kagel would have to see about that later, and get Mr. Bodkin's assurance of foolproof animal discipline, if needed.

So this Bodkin and the woman he teamed with went into the wild after crooks and degenerates. Outlaws targeted by this duo were usually caught, it sounded like. The reports stated the quarry was often some really bad creepers: child slave traders, death cult weirdos, assassins, saboteur commandos, terrorists. People who operated, traveled, fled and hid in impenetrable natural cover. The dense woods, the marshland. Stuff a lot of soldiers didn't even want to navigate. City cops were helpless in it, even the departments across America who were trying to play Green Beret nowadays, with all their military gear. City cops, suburban police departments, playing Rambo. Preposterous. Kagel supposed that's why many of the departments hired Bodkin and his lady friend when it was time for the rubber to meet the road. Help us, please. By any means necessary.

That was another thing. Often this Bodkin individual and the woman, whatever her name was, were hired to bring in especially threatening targets dead or alive.

Seemed like something out of the past, but bounty hunters could still roll that way, apparently. Wanted, dead or alive. Imagine that.

Sometimes the fugitives did in fact end up dead, at least according to the briefings he'd perused. In some cases the executed were freaks who'd rape and killed kids, or sold them to buyers who'd do the same. Others who'd been vanquished were escaped killers: professional and mass murderers, biker gang executioners, and so forth. That would certainly redefine the meaning of "hunting dangerous game." Irwin Kagel kept paging through the collection of printouts.

Yet more gems of humanity taken down by Bodkin and his partner were people who aimed to commit terroristic sabotage, such as making entire municipal water supplies radioactive or choked with biological contaminants. None of these saboteurs had been brought in alive. None. Danger made to disappear. Abracadabra. Kagel savored a bit of rum on his tongue, considering that last fact with approval.

The Bodkin guy sounded like he had an itchy trigger finger. As did the woman: the info here stated that she had more kills than Bodkin. Name? Something *Moreau* maybe…nope, right on the next page her name again appeared. Montrose. Gladdis Montrose. She was described briefly as "shooting expert."

And also categorized in the rundown as *lethal,* just like Bodkin. Kagel noticed that the fed reports stated that word a second time. Significant, since it was not that common for bounty hunters to be mortally dangerous, actually. Maybe the authors of these facts sheets were exaggerating here. Right?

Then Kagel came to the section in the printouts where the New Orleans activities were discussed. The federal agents' summary statement, wrapping up the briefing on this Lee Bodkin guy's assignment in storm-ravaged New Orleans.

The big picture was one of small-time thugs retaining or stealing plenty of guns, and looting, robbing, and killing to their hearts' content. At the expense of the city's beleaguered common folk, the weak, the injured.

In that spirit, the City of New Orleans, and especially its Superdome, was made into a genuine house of horrors by the strongest – i.e., most well-armed – gangs in town.

And the brutality didn't stop with residents of the city. The ruffians extended the thieving and beatings to volunteers who rushed to the city to help. They also greeted some of those volunteers with murder.

Based on the reports, the murders of these health care workers and first responders served as the catalyst to push the Feds to drop all restraint. It had been the final factor resulting in this protective pair and their dog being brought into the mess. Two people and a dog against, as the fact sheet stated, "a minimum of twenty perpetrators."

At this point in the tale, Kagel wished he could have found out more. The reports were too brief. To him, a guy who always needed physical protection and rescue from harm, it was…was…entrancing. Kagel wiped a small smile from his face, took another taste of rum, then sampled a little more reading. Plenty of commentary in the printouts describing the event, but the crux of the matter locked in Kagel's focus.

So many facts and official storytelling had been imbedded into the report. But none stood out more than how this dynamic duo, Bodkin and Montrose, addressed the "minimum of twenty" homicidal bad guys.

Suspected aggressors *were herded into dense cover,* where the threat was then removed. That was verbatim from the report.

Kagel had to read that line again.

The remaining gang members had been forced into the swamp. And the threat was removed. The authors of the report went on.

The team reached their objective by using precision bullet placement to contain the targets, and also by implementing the assistance of "canine resources." To "herd" the murderers where they wanted them to go. Via the tactics of a sharpshooter and an attack dog.

But the report left out something obvious. After the creeps ran into the swamp, how was the "threat" exactly "removed"? It appeared that someone had been in there, waiting for the scumbags. A shotgun enthusiast who also happened to be an expert in hand-to-hand combat? A veteran of thick cover maneuvers? For a person who could kill wild deer up close using Paleolithic cra archery equipment...how much challenge would out-of-shape, untrained thugs be, in thick brush no less? Kagel could guess who the person awaiting the thugs was, and what basically had happened.

Bad people snuffed out. Tough. Sometimes, you mess with the bull, you get the horns. Kagel guessed he was going to like this armed duo for hire. He felt himself smiling again. He sipped a little more of the brown liquor.

To sum it all up, according to the Feds' database rundown: two guns for hire, people who could stalk prey. Neither had been military, not officially at least. Although it looked to Kagel like they were in fact soldiers in a certain respect. Or professional hunters. Predators for money, but not assassins. Special ops on a budget, you could say.

Not fanatics. They each made a living with endeavors separate from their being hired out for the violent apprehension tasks. The woman was an outdoor survival expert, and held wilderness retreats every season of the year in Minnesota. Even in winter. And at a hefty price tag for her students. And once again, Bodkin was reputed to be a craftsman of that historic-style archery equipment. So money was present regardless of the manhunt stuff for both of them. Bodkin and Montrose didn't just do this to make a quick buck.

Not real gentle folks, these two. Sometimes the targets they chased were killed. In Kagel's current dilemma, that eventuality would work out splendidly.

The Bodkin guy was in town now; it was Kagel's only chance. But would an intrepid he-man, as Kagel imagined this gun-for-hire guy to be, even consider joining up with a small, slight, old guy like him? A dweeb like the scientific, fastidious Irwin Kagel? And be willing to work with a partner like Ragnor?

Time would tell. But no time to waste. Action had to be taken soon. But how to approach such a gun-for-hire? Dealing with such hombres was way out of Kagel's field of expertise.

Kagel didn't know it yet, but his luck was about to change. For the better. Because it wouldn't be long before he talked with Lee Bodkin. Because Bodkin would soon be in need of help. And he'd be coming to Irwin Kagel to get it.

7

"Would you like me to cue the violin serenade here?" Lee Bodkin said. He cradled the cell phone between shoulder and ear while digging into the bag of trail mix. Looked like there were two M&Ms left.

"Don't make light of it, Bodkin," Gladdis Montrose said. "You yourself have had some rough patches after a shooting. Emotional roller coaster and all that. When that's happened, I've been there to weather the storm, right along with you."

Following their latest assignment in Wisconsin, Montrose had been stricken with a dose of post-trauma. Rare, especially for her, but it had happened occasionally over the years. The outing had been a mostly smooth project, done by the book with their typical strategies progressing nicely. Then Gladdis Montrose killed both of the suspects.

They'd been chasing a couple of killers. Both were hitmen who'd been working for crooked career politicians in D.C. The assassins had just been hired for another murder, to take place at a Wisconsin lodge. Out of the killers' comfort zone, way out of their element in the woods, and right into the waiting talons of Bodkin and Montrose. Oh my.

The previous job the two degenerates had carried out was the eliminating of some political liabilities: innocents who knew too much, more or less. Then, the next day, they'd murdered a barista at a D.C. coffee shop, while she worked. She'd recently been pressured by a warped politico – one of the guys who employed the killers, and a "respected" member of the House of Representatives, no less – to perform sexual improprieties while serving as an intern. The young woman refused, and things got aggressive. She was to turn state's evidence next month. Unfortunately for her, she was also slated to be taken out by assassins before that could happen.

So, overall, the .243-caliber slugs from the rifle Montrose fired were basically avenging angels. Better than the pricks deserved, Bodkin believed. But, those two acts of killing were the straws that made cracks in the conscience of Gladdis Montrose. Bodkin knew firsthand that it's not easy killing people if you're not a sociopath. Or not a career politician, for that matter.

To neutralize the threat, Gladdis acted in typical form with her bolt action weapon: two shots, two kills. Preemptive fire actually, before either guy could squeeze off shots from the guns they'd pointed her way.

Two dead sadists, no problem, Bodkin figured. Besides, it was easier rolling their bodies from the woods with a high-wheel deer cart when they'd assumed dead status. The cold weather made the carcass situation a bit more pleasant as well. In that case, frozen solid was good.

There was no point in his reassuring Gladdis that each shooting had been a righteous kill. They were so far past those rookie doubts that he and Gladdis never even spoke about the subject. Lots of notches in a gun's stock didn't make playing the role of executioner any easier for the soul to digest, though.

"Yes, true," Bodkin said, continuing the conversation. "You've been there as a pillar of support for me, no doubt. A short one, but a strong one," Bodkin said, picturing her frame, tall in stature but short in height, a fraction under 5'1".

"Ha ha."

"Although I do recall you using some shaming language."

"What would you do in my case, with a despondent lump of muscle hunched over a table in front of me, seeking solace in a bottle of White Zinfandel?" Montrose said.

"Got me there. I do appreciate the encouragement over the years, of course. But what's with the shaming? Is that what a good counselor would do?" Bodkin asked.

"What 'shaming' are you referring to exactly?" Montrose said.

"Stuff like 'come on, you big wuss.'"

"If I remember correctly, that particular shaming was over your usual choice of drink, Lee. You know, there are genuine wines out there for sale."

"Yeah, but none so reassuring. White Zin reminds me of the Kool-Aid I chugged as a kid, only it has plenty of alcohol to enhance the effects."

"Sweet as cotton candy, too. You're a real connoisseur, Bodkin."

Bodkin switched the cell phone to his other ear. He could hear the strain in her voice through the phone: throat seizing a little bit, more effort than usual in her enunciation. His partner wasn't as well with the world yet as she was pretending.

"No need to tell you, you're going to have a hard time overcoming this funk if you can't sleep," Bodkin said.

"Suggest some kind of sleep aid?" Montrose said.

"No, that stuff is usually a bad idea. Best to try something natural. Maybe…"

"Beat you to it," Montrose said. "Tonight Gunther's coming over. With his massage table. He promised one hour, full-body."

"Is that the German guy from the university? The one with the whole Fabio thing going on?" Bodkin asked.

"His hair's now styled in a more modern fashion."

"What happened to Pogo?"

"You mean Pablo?"

"Oh yeah," Bodkin said. "Him."

"You looking to shift into chaperone work, Lee?" Montrose said.

"Heavens no." Bodkin had a girlfriend of his own, and was in no position to feel it, but a pinch of jealousy seemed to flirt inside him. "But, really," he said. "How many guys do you keep in reserve?"

"A whole stringer, Lee. I'll let you go."

"Pissed?"

"Oh no. Your humor attempts are putting me to sleep. This could be my chance to drift off," Montrose said.

Bodkin was about to end the call, when Montrose said, "Hey." With more urgency all of a sudden.

"Still here," Bodkin said.

"That thing you touched on about locals being edgy because of some killings," Montrose said.

"Yes, that they are. No worries, though. Not for me, anyway," Bodkin said.

"Can't be too careful. I assume you're rolling with some accoutrements," Montrose said.

"Just the hand cannon."

"The .40 or the revolver?"

"Revolver. Fillet knife, too. And rapier wit," Bodkin said.

"I'd put little faith in that last one," Montrose said. "Sheba doing fine?"

"Perfect. Well-nourished too, with all the food she's been stealing from me," Bodkin said.

"Stealing? I actually picture her guilt tripping, and you being weak and giving in."

"Like always," Bodkin said.

"If this situation materializes into a real threat, and you decide to help the town council or whomever, count me in," Montrose said.

"Easy there, my dear. Probably turn out to be some imbalanced loner or something. Going nuts after maybe chugging moonshine and sniffing gasoline," Bodkin said. "Thanks, but I'm not concerned."

She was in no psychological condition to tackle this type of weird swamp stalker scenario, Bodkin knew. Even if Bodkin was signing on, he'd keep Gladdis Montrose out of it. This time at least.

"You plan on some wandering around in the wilds while down there?" Montrose said.

"Naturally. As a matter of fact, just after sunrise tomorrow morning, I'm heading down the beach to where a creek empties into the sea. A robust run of spotted sea trout should be commencing. Plan to acquire some trout slabs."

"Good eating?"

"I intend to find out," Bodkin said.

"Well, just keep a heads up."

"And you rest up."

"Keep me posted, buddy," Montrose said.

"See you in a week," Bodkin said.

8

Nothing teaches a lesson like failure. The creature had failed in this spot several times, and accordingly had learned plenty. But the failure would stop today. Success and conquest would take its place.

The creature didn't have a sophisticated plan, but it didn't need one. The targeted prey, the small humans, should come back to this location again today. Just like yesterday, in that big, noisy, rolling yellow shelter. The creature had waited several times, while watching the prey, for some of them to leave that yellow shelter and come in his direction. Where he could grab one or more of them.

But the young prey never did. In the very simplistic, instinctive recesses of its mind, the reality of the prey's lack of wandering was surprising to the creature. Most infant and yearling animals of other species – pigs, deer, rabbits – wandered about recklessly until either being reined in or nearly abandoned by their elders. These young specimens here, however – the human hatchlings – were reluctant to stray. Instead, they just left the yellow shelter's cover and ran directly into their protective lair, the even larger abode that sat across the creek from where the creature now sat. The human hatchlings did this as if obeying some kind of orders, and facing some kind of punishment for not doing so.

The creature was frustrated by this. It too, in its early years, had endured rules, tests, lessons. Punishment too. Per the requirement forced upon it to obey its masters. Those days were now gone, and the creature was determined to keep it that way. But for its potential victims, the obedience factor seemed apparent, as they rushed into the shelter so quickly every time. Obeying and thus complicating the creature's current mission.

But, as always, due to those early influences and training sessions in its life – as well as to its unique genetics – the creature immediately focused on alternatives. Stewing on disappointments was a secondary urge at best, whereas finding actions leading to success was first.

Actions, yes. Here was the creature's simple action plan.

Surge forth and acquire. Stop watching from afar and waiting for a victim to come its way. Go forward. Pursue. Grasp success and satisfaction. By grabbing a human hatchling, satisfaction would surely be the result. Smash, pummel, bite. The creature could barely wait.

Was the strategy safe? No. But no matter. The creature was influenced, seduced really, by thoughts of mayhem, by the thrill of the kill. Also by the nutrients it would acquire. And as a tradeoff for the assertive approach, all safety would be on the line here.

Forget caution, the primitive brain of the creature urged itself. Risk it all. Risk discovery. Risk failure. Risk dangerous humans interceding, as they carried and used those gun tools against him. The creature would deal with any human beings who interfered, as need be. Deal with them using ferocious retribution. Its usual.

The action plan's specifics: rush the moving yellow shelter once it stopped, and as the targeted prey emerged, acquire the ultimate attack position. To hurtle onto its prey from above.

With a running start, leaping to the top of the shelter would be basic for the creature. If the sides of the shelter proved to be too slippery, it could acquire a handhold by using one of the many openings along the shelter's side…the openings the little human hatchlings kept sticking their hands and faces out of as the yellow shelter came and left.

The creature wouldn't wait until the entire group had exited the yellow shelter…just some of them. With half of them out and half of them still inside, the key moment would present itself. Although the creature had no words to describe the situation, it knew the confusion and lack of awareness would be greatest for the victims at that instant. The pandemonium of the hatchlings scrambling, pushing, and scurrying from the shelter's security, as they always did, would result in a prime opportunity for the creature. Their confusion was key. And if the ones outside of the yellow shelter proved too evasive somehow, there'd still be plenty left inside.

Death from above. If the furry predator had known how to smile, it would have.

The creature hunkered down in the moist greenery, feeling the rays of the rising sun, listening to the gurgling creek, peering through the brush. Waiting for the noisy yellow shelter, full of human hatchlings, to appear.

Anticipating the moment the old school bus would rumble up into position.

9

Bodkin opened his eyes. Early morning. Time to wake up with the sun. A new day, a new adventure. Seize the day! Whatever.

He'd slept several hours…what, almost six? Could have used more, a lot more. Deep fatigue was far from cleared. Grogginess remained.

Last night Bodkin had spent a couple of hours staring at the ceiling before zonking out. Sleep had again evaded him. Perhaps because of the ghosts of the assignment they'd just wrapped up? A new, unfamiliar atmosphere? Maybe a strange bed? Bodkin couldn't settle on a definite reason.

Didn't matter. He was in Florida now. Time was slipping away.

Get up.

Dog nuggets for Sheba, a Clif Bar for himself. Then a Power Bar. Both washed down with mediocre coffee from the room's brewer, but the java bolstered by putting in two packets of grounds instead of just one. All the subtleties and satisfaction of a molasses and motor oil mix. Yum. Down the hatch.

What grogginess?

Before he knew it, he'd retrieved the fishing rod and tiny tackle pouch from his truck. Sun already up, but the fish should still be feeding. Gotta get going.

And soon they were. Man, wolf-dog, fishing rod, and a container of small, shiny lures, strolling along Chicola's beachfront. Along with a shiny, razor-like fillet knife in its sheath, slid into Bodkin's front pocket. Plus a heavy, large-caliber revolver stuck into the waistband of his jeans, snugged in at the small of his back.

Heading for the creek that ran just past an elementary school. Ready for action. Anticipating spotted sea trout steaks.

***

The creature rose slightly from its crouch. With the sounds of creaking metal and a choking engine, the big yellow shelter thing rolled in the creature's direction. The repulsive small humans could be seen as they jumped around inside of the yellow shelter like so many tumbling leaves. The noise of their chatter already reached the creature. Soon they'd spill from the yellow enclosure, in motion, running and playing, unaware completely about what was coming for them. The creature was full of anticipation.

Ready for action. Anticipating dead human hatchlings. Lots of them.

***

Ah, the correct creek. This was the fourth stream they'd come upon, and it was by far the heaviest flowing. Looking to his right, Bodkin could in fact see the roof of a single story building over the top of the sandy, brushy bank. That must be the grade school.

Water repellent fishing shoes in place, Bodkin stepped into the cool current of the creek. A pair of swirls in the water surged near him, and a tail swished at the surface. Alarmed fish, large ones, not minnows, heading back up the creek. Bodkin's excitement surged along with the flourish of the escaping trout.

Bodkin heard the approach of a rumbling truck, or maybe a school bus. Several buses probably arrived at the school each morning, dumping a load of scrambling kids, then returned later to scoop them back up. It hadn't occurred to Bodkin earlier, but it dawned on him now: his presence so close to the property of a school may seem out of place. Or maybe even against the law. For all he knew, the creek was actually on official school grounds, legally. He obviously wasn't faculty or staff. Should he still proceed?

Of course. In situations like this, Bodkin had long ago decided right or wrong was determined by a person's being detected or not. He calculated that in this setting he could avoid detection.

The creek entered what looked like an impenetrable mass of tree trunks, vines, brush, and hanging Spanish moss. He'd stay in the thickness, down in the creek's little ravine, and blend. Accordingly, Sheba was also an expert at the low profile maneuver.

Bodkin heard another fish swirl, and all doubt vanished. He and Sheba proceeded up the creek, toward the concentration of ravenous fish. Along the bank that led behind the elementary school.

***

It would clear the creek with one leap. Then the creature would bound forward a few more times and spring atop the enclosure that had arrived with the stinking little humans. It would slam down upon its victims and begin its destruction. The creature planned to take as many as it could.

The yellow shelter rested in place now, grumbling and shaking. The human hatchlings babbled and shouted as they spilled from it. The creature rose from its crouch, and slipped forward without a sound to the bank of the creek. Ready to attack now, it rose from all fours to stand on two legs.

As the creature had lain in wait this morning, breezes had wafted across its hiding spot off and on. From the ocean's direction, bringing scents of seaweed, salt, and musty swamp moisture from the wetland nearest the beach. Now, another breeze brushed past the creature, just one second after it had risen up.

The creature bent over in a crouch, alarm arcing through its system. It went back down to all fours, cowering. It looked in the direction from which the breeze had drifted, across the section of forest before the beach began. After examining that area, the creature saw nothing new. Then it glanced down, into the wedge that formed the creek bottom.

Intruders!

Picking their way along the water's edge, peering into the creek. As if hunting the fish in there. A bulky human thing, male, almost its own size, accompanied by some kind of wolf beast. The canine was slender and much lighter in weight than the human, in the creature's crude estimation. The canine wolf thing did not alarm the creature, not much anyway. The human thing, though, did...that thick frame, the movement and posture. It wasn't typical of the creature's ideal prey. The way the male human moved summoned discomfort deep inside the creature. The human appeared to be something that preyed on other things. Something that stalked.

Instincts from thousands of years of its ancestors' development triggered the feelings. These emotions had been tweaked by its training in earlier stages of its life. With weak, vulnerable opponents, it had been taught to take them head-on and immediately. Don't hesitate. With stronger, perhaps superior prey, consider evasion. Escape. Avoidance. Live to fight another day.

Or instead, take that strong prey by surprise.

Which in this case meant: assault the male human first, without warning, disable it. Then immediately smash and eliminate the canine beast. Go back to the disgusting human. Finish that larger one off as fast as possible, then return to the engaging of little human hatchlings. Maybe return to the bulky male human and the canine following the execution of the hatchlings, the skulls of these larger enemies being the focus. Feed on them and leave them. That last thought, spurred by urgent cravings, was the tipping point. The creature hungered, it thirsted.

Yes. Yes. Go.

***

Bodkin saw the largest trout yet; it had just sucked down a little bug at the surface of the creek, then vanished. Time for his first cast. He turned to Sheba to check if she'd also seen the swirl, as he unhooked the small gold-colored spinner from the fishing rod's cork handle.

Sheba was looking elsewhere. Up the embankment. Bodkin heard some rustling, some kind of crushing of small twigs into mud. Like a heavy person, or thing, would make. An uncertain stench drifted into his nostrils: sweat, feral life form, filth. The very start of a growl rumbled in Sheba's throat. Then the dark bulk flew from the brush above, straight for him.

***

The creature's brain screamed with killing lust as it lunged on all fours to the edge of the bank, past the weeds, in clear view of the human rubbish below and its wolf partner. It flung itself into the air, aiming for the human, intending to hit its body with both surprise and force. Before it left the plateau, it took in what the human held in its hand…just a play thing, a toy, some kind of skinny stick. The human was defenseless. *Kill it.*

The creature hit the muddy bank, no human flesh beneath it as anticipated. The human scum had evaded it…the mongrel human had twirled in a roll onto the ground or something. The creature's flying fist, meant to pulverize the man-thing's face, had missed. Instead, it had snapped the play thing stick in two. The human had dropped the half stick it held, and was now on its feet, facing the creature. Easy kill. *Do it, now.*

In an instant, the wolf thing was on its arm, biting. The creature screamed, flailing the arm, launching the canine through the air. Back to the male human. *Kill it.*

The vile human…held a thunder maker! The thunder maker – an implement for the dread of which the creature had scalded into its brain as a toddler, as soon as it could stand.

Training in the early days emphasized nothing more urgent. The thunder maker meant death. Rewards were given for avoiding them, punishment for disregarding them. And for not eliminating them. *Smite the thunder maker!*

A half-second after seeing the gun, the thunder maker, the creature leapt forward, leaving the muddy ground. A swipe of the creature's arm, with a fury intended to smash the thunder maker and break bone, made the shiny thunder maker fly from the human scum's hand. The human looked down, ready to pick the weapon back up from the ground.

The creature burst into the enemy human male, head first, the top of its cranium slamming into the human's gut. An audible exhalation assured the creature. It came up flailing a fist with murderous fury, connecting with the disgusting human's face. It then went for the smash and bite on the human, who now lay on the soft ground.

Not to be, not yet. The human was back up on its feet. Its weak, horrid body again stood in front of the creature. It had rolled and flipped, faster than the creature could follow. The creature was not accustomed to this. Other human victims had surrendered so easily. The human crouched, and now brandished the upper half of its skinny stick toy. No worry at all to the creature. It told itself as much, as a different emotion was starting to well up inside it. The lightning bolt of doubt.

The human's other hand reached into its lower body garment, just as the canine leapt to the creature's face. The creature clutched the wolf thing, again pitching it into the brush. Back to the male human.

The human now had a shiny talon in its hand, for which the creature had rudimentary training. Sharp, dangerous, but no match for the creature when in full rage mode. The creature moved forward, eager to smash. To bite.

Except. Like a wasp on its left forearm, then a hornet in its right eye, then a hard rock tossed into its face…the creature had a slice on its arm, had the fishing rod tip jammed into its eye, had a human foot slammed into its nose. Then the canine hit again, this time onto the back of the creature's neck, going for the bottom of its head. The creature screamed and rolled into the weeds, flipping the canine off it.

Up again, facing the human. But the creature couldn't move forward. The skinny stick toy, the end of which had just poked its eye, was swishing through the air. With rhythm. The motion was complemented by the human's other arm, which held the shiny talon tool.

Nothing to worry about, the creature had been trained thus…yet a glance down confirmed the talon tool had sliced the creature's arm. Red blood specks dripped down from the creature's forearm to the weeds below, spattering in delicate crimson stars on the leaves.

The male human did not retreat. The creature was being thrown off its game. The canine was approaching again, it could hear the slender animal from behind.

The human advanced. Advanced! Against the creature! The skinny stick in one hand, the talon blade in the other. The objects in its hands in constant motion, like stinging insects moving in figure eights, impossible to follow, the motion hypnotizing, terrifying in its menace. The creature locked eyes with the stinking human male, and what it saw there was worse than anything else…the human wasn't afraid.

The canine wolf thing was on the creature again, now at its legs. The creature slammed a fist into the canine again and again, forcing the fanged thing away. While distracted, the creature let its guard down, allowing the human to step forward. The skinny stick toy the human held whipped into the creature's face, then sought its eyes again.

The creature bellowed, and before it realized what it was doing, it had begun retreating. Shameful, impossible to fathom up until this moment. But it had no time to consider. The canine was after the creature, teeth bared, and the human advanced as well. Beyond belief.

Then the human changed directions, backpedaling away. With that, space had been made between the creature and the human, too much for the creature to now connect with a single leap. The man-thing first dropped the skinny stick it held, then the shiny talon, the blade.

The human crouched down and swept up the thunder maker, eyes already acquiring the creature as its target.

***

"Party time, motherfucker," Bodkin said. The sights of the .357 magnum were on the dark, furry bulk, then the bulk was gone. Up and over the wall of the creek bank, with a screech. Sheba burst up the embankment after it.

Then Bodkin burst up the embankment after it.

Dodging through ferns, saplings, branches, vines. Bodkin glimpsed Sheba ahead, snapping, making contact with the attacker thing. The freaky beast shrieked again, and beast and dog were both gone into the dark greenery.

Run. Dodge, duck, scramble, run, run.

Into a clearing where Sheba had the furry thing at bay, the dog moving in half circles, left then right, a lunge forward, then a lunge back. The furry monster thing was hunched in a ready position, taking swings at Sheba when she moved in, missing each time.

The shaggy demon looked down at the attacking dog, ready to take another swipe. Then up at Bodkin, just as the iron sights of the heavy revolver lined up with the top of its chest. Right in the center, above the creature's pectorals.

With a roaring squeal, the hairy shape whirled and sprung to the tree trunk behind it, the turning of its back to the canine allowing one last snap to its leg. Then it was up, with a single push, out of Sheba's reach, 10 feet, maybe 12, then up to 18 feet, soon 25 feet, then gone.

In just over one second. Far too fast to lock in with the handgun for a killing shot.

Bodkin held the gun in full ready position, ready for a sudden return. Half a minute later, he lowered the weapon to relaxed but ready. Two more minutes, Bodkin let the .357 dangle at his side. All the while listening for breaking or bending branches, brush crunching in the thickness, the thudding into the ground of a return charge.

No such sounds. Sheba looked up the tree into which the thing had escaped. Then to the ones beyond it, then to the jungle-like growth in front of them. Bodkin knew his dog well enough to recognize that she had no clue where the attacker thing now was.

Bodkin's heaving breath had now evened out. Sweat ran over the spot on his face where the furball with teeth had smacked him. An abrasion there let in some of the salt, stinging the wound. Before this moment, perspiration had barely had time to start: the whole confrontation had lasted less than two minutes. Bodkin considered what he had seen. All observations were unsettling.

The thing had fangs, large ones, like a carnivore.

The freak was as big as Bodkin himself.

The fucker knew how to punch.

Lightning fast. If not faster than Sheba, that thing was close.

It had known what a gun was.

Other thoughts churned in the back of Bodkin's mind as he tried to grasp the sudden brawl…particularly, other words: rogue bear, monster, werewolf. Ogre. Also those words used in local rumors, featuring favorite terms of extraterrestrial buffs: Sasquatch. Bigfoot.

What the hell was that thing?

10

"You don't need to go all the way up to Tallahassee for it," said Chief of Police Ernest Felton. "Resources for you, and for your dog, can be found a lot closer than that."

Lee Bodkin looked at Felton and waited. No more pointers were forthcoming, so Bodkin inquired further.

"Well, if you could recommend a veterinarian around here, that would be great. But distance isn't the main issue. I'll go as far as needed."

"I appreciate the concern you have for your dog, buddy. But let's collect some facts first. Your dog has been cut, or maybe bitten. You yourself are working on a pretty good shiner on that one eye, I can see," Chief Felton said. "So what or who attacked you exactly?"

"It happened pretty fast," Bodkin said, returning to one of his usual tactics: lying in the face of authority. It was a skill Bodkin had long ago perfected, and found as valuable for survival as any other. "Just a blur, some big dark shape flew at us and attacked Sheba. Then it was gone."

"A wild boar, possibly. Pigs are all over back in the swamp," Felton said.

"Yeah, that might have been it," Bodkin lied.

Felton continued looking at Bodkin, as if waiting for the truth.

"So you can help us?" Bodkin said.

"Shouldn't be a problem, son. I'll make a call to one of my contacts. He'll get your animal all repaired and healthy," Felton said. "But one thing first, if I may change the subject. We've got a local problem. A menace, actually. One which I think you may have come in contact with. Maybe during this recent misadventure."

"Not sure I follow, sir," Bodkin said.

"Our department was wondering if your services are available. For the week, at least."

This again. "Not looking for work of any kind. Thanks anyway, though. Just want to get on with the dog's medical needs and continue my vacation here," Bodkin said.

Chief Felton and another, younger cop stood facing Bodkin in the lobby of the small, clean police station. In Bodkin's estimation, Felton was maybe in his late 50s. He was also heavily built, wide at the waist as well as the shoulders, and outwardly macho. As he stood square to Bodkin, Felton hitched his thumbs into his black leather belt, and made a point to hold his arms out a little more than any muscle required. He held his chin up, a hint of a sneer on his face. Very much like a cowboy gunslinger itching for a fight. Out here in the green swampland, ready for a showdown with anyone who doubted his word.

Felton's face had probably been hard once, but with getting older and gaining maybe an extra 30 pounds or so since those days, his countenance had more of the pumpkin look. Bodkin had to watch out for that himself, especially once he got to Felton's age. Bodkin currently had the block jaw look, but there were no guarantees with the passage of time. No one would know what his face featured underneath if it got covered with swollen layers of softness. Yep, to avoid the Chief Felton look, he'd have to keep an eye on his excessive intake of pizza as the years rolled on. As well as spaghetti noodles. And apple fritters.

Bodkin noticed the hair dye Felton had chosen: that light brown/reddish coloration that older guys had started to adorn graying hair with over the past decade. Not realistic at all. The chief had even touched up his military-issue moustache with the ink. In Bodkin's opinion, if a guy was going to dye his hair, he should maybe use a color that actually existed within humankind. Just Bodkin's opinion, of course, and apparently not Felton's.

The other, younger cop had short, jet black hair – looked natural in color – brushed straight back, dark eyes to match, Caucasian skin turned brownish-orange from the sun. Or from a tanning salon. He'd either had his teeth whitened, or he'd stuck bright white breath mints in the front of his mouth for the same effect.

"So, nothing we can do to get you to consider helping out?" Felton said. "To discuss the option of teaming up?"

"There must be some misunderstanding. Teaming up? I'm just down here as a frozen Northerner looking for some reprieve from the cold," Bodkin said. "Infusing your town with my money. In exchange for a little sun."

"We looked into you, my friend. With your background, we believe you can come to the rescue here," Felton said.

"I think you've got the wrong guy," Bodkin said.

Felton watched Bodkin for a moment, chewing a piece of skin inside his mouth gently, kind of like nibbling at a toothpick, Bodkin thought. This Florida policeman really seemed to wish he were John Wayne.

"Oh yeah? Then let's see some ID," Felton said. The slick-haired officer behind him smirked upon the chief's statement. The mouth of the young cop opened up with the partial smile…yep, real teeth. Quite brilliant as the fluorescent lights of the lobby caught them and made them glimmer, Bodkin noticed. Nice. Almost like nature had intended.

Felton himself re-hitched his thumbs in his belt, and his arms suddenly stuck out a bit more from his body, as if a very quick increase in upper back size had just commenced.

Hardball. Oh boy. Bodkin remained quiet, and made no attempt to produce any identification. He looked directly into Felton's eyes, a neutral gaze telling nothing, then at the smug officer next to Felton. Then back to the chief.

"I believe you know who I am," Bodkin said.

"We think we do, too. Yet you're trying to pass yourself off as some simple tourist."

"No, in fact, I'll readily admit I'm a paid man hunter and tracker, and currently not on the job. I'm now in your town of Chicola, simply seeking some R and R," Bodkin said.

"R and R, huh? That's a military expression, you know," Felton said. He peered at Bodkin. In return, Bodkin said nothing.

"Not sure you have the right to use it, seeing as you never even served," said the cop standing there with Felton.

Bodkin raised his eyebrows and waited.

"Why didn't you? The armed forces too regimented for you? Or some kind of problem with authority?" the bright-toothed cop said.

"Not really, as an answer to either. Just selfish, independent, and bullheaded," Bodkin said. "In my younger days, besides attending class and working, I pretty much wanted to just fish, hunt, and wrestle."

"And it paid off for your career, we see," said the younger cop.

"How so, officer?" Bodkin said. No provocation in his tone, but a purposeful absence of any interest as he asked it. Bodkin even looked back at Felton, not at the other cop, to emphasize his lack of concern over the answer.

"You drive an old Chevy pickup beater for one thing. Old, green, fading bucket of bolts, looks like. Doesn't speak real well of your position in society, pal."

"Uh, well," Bodkin replied. "It's a Ford, for one thing. The transmission is a rebuilt one from the supply they use in NASCAR service trucks. You know, the kind they use to tow a dozen cars at once. And all the bolts, on the frame at least, are quasi-titanium. So that makes for one solid bucket of bolts." Bodkin then winked at the younger cop.

"Huh. All I know is, we don't like Chicola filled with old junkers. Our staff here makes a conceited effort to keep up appearances," the cop said.

"You mean concerted," Bodkin said.

The cop stuck his head forward, as if trying to imitate a Canadian goose about to strike. The energy was off, though; his version of a goose looking perhaps like one struck with the flu.

"Excuse Lieutenant Kort, here," Felton said to Bodkin. "He was in the U.S. Army, just like me. He's proud of it, and rightfully so."

"Sure, makes sense," Bodkin said. "Now, about that animal hospital…I can't leave it to chance if my pet acquires an infection or not."

"And we're proud of our military service for a reason," Kort continued. "We were trained, had to prove ourselves. We're not thugs chasing ambulances, so to speak. Hearing of problems, then showing up conveniently to take over." He locked Bodkin with a stare, a menacing one, or at least an attempt at such.

"I don't follow," Bodkin said.

"People start getting killed here, and you just happen to show," Kort said. "Pretty coincidental."

"I'm not in town because of any killings or other crimes. I'm here to bask, rest, and maybe swim. And to eat," Bodkin said.

"And I maintain it's quite a coincidence," Kort said.

"Easy, Kevin," Felton said to Mr. Shiny Teeth. He turned back to Bodkin. "So, Mr. Bodkin is in fact your name, I can safely conclude."

Bodkin gave a third of nod, as if performing the slightest imitation of a bow.

"Lee Bodkin?"

"The one and only," Bodkin said.

"Wonderful," Felton said. "A bounty hunting celebrity, right in our humble little town."

"Yeah right, Chief. We're actually being graced with the presence of a great pretender," Kort said. "A guy who picks up a shotgun, buys a dog, and talks some blonde sidekick into traveling with him, can call himself anything. Even a bounty hunting professional."

"What big things did you do in the Army, anyway?" Bodkin said, looking at Kort.

"Special Forces," Kort said.

Bodkin wasn't surprised. Weren't most ex-military guys, regardless of whatever menial roles they played in the service, suddenly "Special Forces" years later?

"What division?" Bodkin said.

Kort hesitated, cast half a glance at Felton, then said, "Army Rangers."

"Couldn't make Delta Force?" Bodkin said.

Kort took a step forward. Felton glanced at the ceiling, having seen this before.

"I'll match anyone, toe-to-toe, with tactical maneuvers. Anytime, anywhere," Kort said.

"If that's the case, why is your Sergeant Morton the one about to trudge into the swamp to find this killer?" Bodkin said.

Kort took another step forward, the smirk changing to more of a snarl. The lights above still glimmered off Kort's teeth. Regardless of smile or snarl, quite shiny, Bodkin observed. Impressive.

"Stop it, Kevin. We got stuff to do. Let's move on," Felton said, looking at Kort for a moment, his displeasure evident. Then back to Bodkin. "I'll make a call over to our town's version of an animal doctor. He's not open for service to the public, mind you. But with my recommendation I'm sure he'll make an exception in your case. However, he doesn't really see pets that often."

"Then why's he considered a veterinarian?" Bodkin said.

With this, Chief Felton took in Bodkin again, not liking the fact that his statement had been questioned.

Sigh. Bodkin was tiring of this routine, and this town in general. Maybe he'd try Clearwater next time. Or Sarasota. Go north from there and swim with the manatees or something. Or pull out all the stops and visit West Palm Beach. Right now he needed to get medical attention for Sheba, just as he'd been telling Felton and his fellow cop – he of the chip on the shoulder – Kevin Kort. Not that easy so far.

Bodkin's first stop right after the skirmish with that...that thing...was the Knick Knack Shack, figuring the owner there, uh, Walton was his name, could point him to an animal hospital somewhere nearby. But the shack was closed up, no Walton around. Then, logically, Bodkin thought of the skinny, awkward Sergeant Grady Morton. He'd hopefully be in the police station, but there was no way for Bodkin to know, one way or another. He'd planned to simply go there and find out, figuring the police headquarters in town shouldn't be too hard to find.

Bodkin was right, about the station at least. The station had been easy enough to find, as it was located at the beginning of Main Street. It was the building in best repair along the whole avenue, thus readily noticeable. Bodkin went into the lobby, anticipating that his luck would hold out and Morton would be in the police station.

Morton wasn't. And here Bodkin now stood, with policemen extraordinaire Felton and Kort. And it was looking like the tough guy police chief needed some coddling.

"I just want to make sure this animal doctor knows what he's doing with dogs, that's all. No disrespect meant," Bodkin said.

"None taken," Felton said, surrendering. Again he looked at Lieutenant Kort, as if to imply that was what the subordinate officer should think as well. He returned his attention to Bodkin.

"I don't know every detail about his experience, but trust me, the doctor is more than qualified to treat a dog. I hear he's treated all kinds of animals, wild and domestic."

"Wild?" Bodkin asked.

"Yep, and not just on this continent neither," Felton said.

"You don't say," Bodkin replied, then remained quiet and waited. He started to sense a bit of B.S. from the chief.

"And he runs quite the unique laboratory; it's just down the road leading from town. That facility pays us a handsome pile of taxes each year, and we definitely need it."

Bodkin nodded, thinking about the city employee health insurance plan. And wondered if it covered dental, specifically Lieutenant Kort's polished teeth. Felton kept talking, and Bodkin tuned back in.

"It has some kind of United Nations recognition. Plenty of funding as a result," Felton said.

"United Nations recognition. Meaning…?" Bodkin said.

"I'm not sure exactly," Felton said.

Aren't you the town's police chief?

"But it's definitely part of the organization's bragging rights," Felton continued. "They made sure we in the town's ruling body knew of those credentials when they wanted to build the compound here."

"When was that?"

"Almost four years ago now."

"But the details of those credentials, were, I suppose, kind of secondary," Bodkin said, enlisting one of his schmoozing shrugs. A great way to make people think you were on their side. "As long as they fork over the annual tax they owe. Money talks."

"Bingo, Mr. Bodkin," Felton said. He followed it with a smile. Felton was starting to like this guy. Conversely, Bodkin could hardly believe this cop. Just pay your taxes, and anything goes. But in reality, weren't most police chiefs and sheriffs basically politicians? Keep the people happy, as long as they keep you in charge and in the dough.

"Anyway, thanks for making the contact. I'll call you soon to find out the verdict," Bodkin said.

"One thing before you go, Lee Bodkin. You ever heard of a guy named Terrence Powell?" Felton asked.

"No, don't believe so."

"Good. He's some kind of researcher on natural phenomena, I guess. Coming to town tomorrow."

"Oh," Bodkin said, not wanting to venture any further on the subject. *Who cares who's coming to town?*

"His visit's related to our problems here in the area. This guy, Powell, is heading over from Idaho or somewhere to ask us a bunch of questions."

"Regarding the killings?" Bodkin asked.

"Yeah, that's what he said. He claims we may have some supernatural presence here now." Felton looked over at Kort, who was still busy glowering at Bodkin.

"He thinks we may have a Bigfoot in the area. Like that Sasquatch legend or something," Felton said. He smirked at Kort, who wouldn't look away from Bodkin. No help there, so Felton turned the smirk instead over to Bodkin, looking for a partner in the ridicule of this Powell guy.

Bodkin just held up his hands, palms up. It was as good as any other gesture when you didn't want to commit. "Hopefully we'll be out of the way before the guy gets here. After seeing the vet, and returning to the beach and all," Bodkin said. Felton dropped the smirk, a little disappointment appearing for a second as he realized Bodkin wouldn't commiserate with him. Then he went to machismo again, taking charge.

"So you have no connection with the Powell guy?" Felton said.

"Nope," Bodkin said.

"OK. We'll give the doc a call for you, Mr. Bodkin. You can call us back in an hour and confirm if and when the doctor can fit you in," Felton said.

"Great. Oh, by the way. What's this doctor's name?" Bodkin asked.

"Dr. Kagel," Felton replied. "Dr. Irwin Kagel."

11

"I'm coming down to help," Gladdis Montrose said.

"Let's not overreact here," Lee Bodkin said in return, switching the phone to his other ear. "It was just some furry blob thing. Nothing I can't handle."

"You just told me it belted you and made you see stars," Montrose said.

"And put the hit on me in a way that I woke up down in the mud. You forgot that part. But no biggie, Sheba saved me."

"You also said the weird thing threw Sheba like a Frisbee," Montrose said. "After slicing her with some nasty fangs."

"Uh, yeah, I guess that did happen," Bodkin relented. "But she recovered beautifully."

"Sure she did. That's too close of a call, in my book," Montrose said.

"Well, it's a hostile world. What can you do?" Bodkin said.

"Here's one thing you can do. Tell that Chicola town council and top cop or whomever that we're on for the mission. I'll come down there and we'll finish the job. Find this thing and take it out. Then I'll catch some sun with you."

Bodkin remained quiet for a few seconds. Was she serious? The two of them, Bodkin and Montrose, both exhausted and sleep-deprived. Going after the thing that had bamboozled him and Sheba…some kind of big, husky beast, the size of an NFL running back. Yet, despite its size, able to move like lightning. Bodkin felt gently along the side of his face, palpated the swelling there, on the spot where a sledgehammer of a fist had collided with his cheek and the corner of his eye.

"What are you packing for ammo?" Montrose said.

"One full cylinder," Bodkin said. "Plus one reload."

"Ah, a loaded six-shooter. And six spare bullets. A regular arsenal," Montrose said.

"Plus my fillet knife," Bodkin said.

"Touché," Montrose said.

"How much sleep did you manage last night, girlie?" Bodkin asked.

"Almost four. Rested a little after that though," Montrose said.

Perfect. The two of them could venture forth, with a wounded dog as their tracker, both in a lack-of-sleep delirium, hunting some kind of fierce ape monster. In contrast to them, the monster itself most likely well-rested. And on its own turf, no less. Didn't seem like good odds.

But…of course, the creature thing might run away as they approached, as it may mistake them with their tired, drooping bodies for a brigade of zombies stumbling along. Might work, who knows?

Bodkin shifted on the hotel's twin bed, the 31-year-old box spring at the base of it creaking a little. Sheba looked up from the floor at him, her neck's mobility now somewhat limited by heavy bandaging atop a smattering of stitches. She'd been sound asleep, and startled by the bed's noise. But it was just her master, once again fidgeting. Nothing new here. She put her head back down and let her body return to limpness.

"Well, four hours of sleep is better than only two or three, I guess," Bodkin said. "But, you know, we could always forget about this situation, and I could leave here early under the cover of darkness tomorrow. Just another transient trying out Florida and leaving. The police chief will probably never miss me."

"Earlier you said the thing you encountered was probably the freak that was attacking people down there."

"I insinuated it, didn't come out and say it," Bodkin said.

"But you believe it though, right? What accosted you is probably what beat some people to death in the area," Montrose said.

"And perhaps bit them to death, yes," Bodkin said.

"Don't you want to save innocent lives?"

"There are innocents everywhere. I don't even know anyone here," Bodkin said. "Don't see why it's my responsibility." That last part was only partly true, Bodkin knew. Assuming the killings were going to continue, he could probably save at least a person or two by stepping in. And without a doubt, he could pick up clues and establish signs of the killer's movements, paths, and places of ambush. Even if it was a person doing it, they'd leave behind at least a small trail of their activities. If it was not a human but rather some kind of animal – Bodkin feeling pretty certain it was in fact his furry opponent in the recent skirmish – the clues should be especially copious. If he did nothing more than pinpoint where a given creature of habit moved and hid, he could turn that info over to the cops here. It would give law enforcement a huge head start, then Bodkin could wash his hands of it, guilt-free.

Bodkin occasionally tried to imagine what it would be like to live as a stone-cold killer, no remorse or concern for anyone else. That wasn't him, though, and it made some things harder. Like walking away when you knew you could help.

"We could use the dough, Lee," Montrose said.

"I'm not even sure about what kind of fee they can offer us," Bodkin said. "Plus, we're not hurting for cash that bad. Why the insistence on this assignment?"

"I could use the outing," Montrose said. Bodkin could still hear the duress in her voice over the phone, kind of an exhausted anxiety. He himself perhaps sounded the same, but he couldn't be sure either way. Earlier he figured she needed time off, plenty of sleep, a big break from the bounty hunting craziness. It was occurring now to Bodkin that his initial amateur analysis could have been wrong. Like 180 degrees wrong. Maybe she simply needed to keep feeding her addiction to action.

A-ha, it now seemed more clear. That was likely what the deal was here. Bodkin should have known. It had happened years back to Gladdis, this same kind of foggy, immobilized thing, but so much had taken place since then. If the current situation was like that last major blue funk she had sunk into, the treatment was simple: get Gladdis out in the wilds, tracking, chasing…shooting. Each night after the hunting insanity, she'd probably resume sleeping like a baby. That was how her previous depression episode had went down.

Burst her back into her comfort zone. How Gladdis got her groove back. Not the makings of a typical chick flick, of course. But to each their own. Gladdis was not your typical woman.

"Didn't you say the town had some kind of national funding status?" Montrose said.

"Yeah, that was mentioned by the police chief. Kind of unclear. United Nations, this or that," Bodkin said.

"So there should be some spare change available."

"Well, technically, the funding infusion doesn't go directly to the town, but rather to a big research lab here.

A large, nearly new compound. It's kind of the financial stronghold of the town, in terms of the tax base."

"Did you actually see the compound?"

"Oh, more than saw it. I was inside of it, with Sheba. That's where she got stitched up," Bodkin said. "Which brings up a separate subject. I've got plenty to tell you about that place. Pretty elaborate, impressive in general. And strange."

"I look forward to it. In person though. I've had about enough phone chat for the time being."

"Understood. One quick thing though: that researcher guy did mention how important it was to fix this stalking killer problem. And he opined that the locals had no clue. So he wants it to happen, and he seems to control the town purse strings to some extent. And most importantly, he then clearly stated that he wants us on it. Not the cops."

"So we might be able to get our regular fee," Montrose said.

"Hopefully," Bodkin said. "That said, Gladdis my friend, I have a hunch this might be too soon for you to see action again."

"Look. You think you're safe there? All tired out and venturing about in the greenery to fish the swamp or whatever?"

"Me wandering around in a daze and going fishing. What's new?" Bodkin said.

"Some kind of killing force sulking nearby, and you sharing the forest with it," Montrose said. "Without your usual armaments."

"A really sharp fillet knife though."

"Didn't you tell me just two minutes ago this freaky beast thingy was probably watching a grade school when you came upon it? That it had crept close enough to check out who ran in and out of it?"

"Yeah, that's what it seemed like. As if it was waiting in ambush. Not real comforting to think about what it had planned," Bodkin said. "But that's what the cops are for, despite what this researcher guy, Kagel, thinks. As for me, if the two of us decide not to go through with the hunt, and I stay down here, I really have nothing to worry about. I'll just stick to the motel and the beach."

"Maybe that predator will come after you there," Montrose said.

What?!

"I hadn't thought about that. But the beach is out in the open," Bodkin said.

"So what? Maybe it likes to attack in the wide open."

Wow.

"OK. But I should be able to see the bastard coming, right? I'm confident that there'd be enough time to draw my sidearm on a stretch of beach."

"What if the freak can swim? Gets you from the water, bursting up from the shallows?"

That got Bodkin's attention. *Oh, man.*

"Could a big hairy beast have that ability?" Bodkin asked.

"Beats me. We don't even know what the hell the thing is," Montrose said.

That decided it, dammit. It was on. By joining the local effort, he could make some more money, let Gladdis get her cathartic therapy, and assuage his own guilt. As well as free himself from thoughts of a humanoid coming up from the deep and emerging from the surf, then scrambling over to his lawn chair for another go at him.

That last part would definitely spoil the beach moment.

"I suppose you're right. OK, let's do it. I'm pretty mad about today's attack anyway. Embarrassed kind of."

"You always have to come out on top," Montrose said.

"Or at least not get beat up. The thing clocked me and dropped me into the dirt."

"My turn to play violins?" Montrose said.

"Ha ha. Anyway, yeah. Come on down, we'll get this done. And I'll pay for the plane ticket, blondie."

"Who are you kidding, bub? We'll go half and half."

"Don't insult me, ma'am," Bodkin said. "You know I have my generous side."

"I'll be there tomorrow night. I'll head out just after noon, if possible. But at any rate, flying first class," Montrose said.

"First class?" Bodkin said, the panicked creak in his voice clearly audible.

"Or nothing," Montrose said.

"Um, yes, in that case, half and half sounds splendid," Bodkin said. "What about our balance sheet? These costs add up."

"We'll deduct it as a business expense. C'mon, Lee, you're sounding like an amateur. A miserly one at that."

"I'm all about miserly. You should see the motel I'm at. The Sea Foam."

"The Sea Foam? I can imagine," Montrose said. "The town has a Holiday Inn. Why didn't you just stay there?"

"The Sea Foam Inn was eight dollars less per night," Bodkin said.

"Every dollar counts, right? So where should I book the flight to? Tallahassee or Pensacola?"

"Pensacola may not be the best idea. All the sailors and pilots might start clamoring for you the moment you leave the plane. I'll never get you down to Chicola," Bodkin said.

"Hmm. Young, hot military guys. Not sounding so bad, Bodkin. Maybe Pensacola is the ticket after all," Montrose said.

"You of a mind to track down a killer, or to be a temptress and bad influence on youthful, inexperienced military guys?" Bodkin said.

"Is that a trick question?"

"Maybe it is in fact time I try my hand at chaperone duty," Bodkin said. Partly kidding and flirting, but some serious feelings under it all. He wished there weren't. But there the emotions lingered. And he knew she knew it.

"You can't run these kind of things for me, Lee. You're no longer single."

"But you are, again."

"You make that sound like a bad thing," Montrose said.

"See you in Tallahassee," Bodkin said. Silence between them, for an eight-count. Then, "Glad you're coming down, blondie," Bodkin said.

"Me too. I'll keep you out of trouble, tough guy," Montrose said.

"Likewise."

Click.

12

Bodkin sat on the motel room's aging little bed, leaning against the wall, feeling the exhaustion. Not to mention a swelling face. Sitting there, thinking.

So yes, he'd traveled to the local research compound and met this Dr. Kagel fellow. Dr. Irwin Kagel, veterinarian-in-a-pinch.

As he'd told Gladdis earlier, the compound had appeared solid and flawless. And impressively immaculate. Not to mention subtly strange. For a makeshift animal hospital, the place definitely represented overkill. Since the visit, it was apparent that much more went on inside those compound walls than simply helping injured animals, but Bodkin was still not sure what.

In the course of following the simple directions given by Chief Felton to find the place, Bodkin drove down the highway, leaving town briefly, and there it was on the outskirts of Chicola. The building was obviously of newer construction, nondescript in that way that specialty machine shops and engineering facilities can often be. It had windows placed along the wall of a small front lobby, with a few along the sides of the building. Those latter windows, he'd noted, had been located high up, maybe 14 feet or so. Way above eye level for a person attempting to peek in. But being eye level or not wouldn't have mattered for a peeping tom anyway: every window of the entire compound was smoked an impenetrable black.

A high fence, perhaps 15 feet tall, formed a utility lot for vehicles and machinery on the side of the compound.

Bodkin could see three white vehicles, one a shiny new van, the other two little wagons, parked inside the fenced lot. Each had some kind of official insignia on the side doors, although it was hard to read the lettering from where he stood. Razor wire lined the top of the fence. Made sense: valuable property deserved ruthless protection, at least in Bodkin's mind. The building itself was maybe 40 feet wide and 100 feet deep; not huge, but Bodkin knew from experience plenty could take place in a building that size. Sometimes savory efforts and operations, sometimes ones not so savory.

Had the compound seemed dangerous? Bodkin hadn't thought so; he sensed nothing menacing when taking in the big picture and approaching the front door.

He felt something else though: an electric sense of mystery, you could say. He glanced at Sheba, who moved along as normal, looking relaxed and deadly, despite her wounds. Bodkin searched the dog for signs of caution, of alarm, as they walked to the entrance. None of the usual indications of such, no hairs on end along her back for instance. She did however crane her head a bit forward, her ears standing up in full alert, a general appearance of eagerness coming over her. Something inside the building had her curious.

Before they could even reach the door to ring its buzzer, the front door opened. There Bodkin and Sheba made contact with the brain power of the facility himself. Irwin Kagel greeted them in person, no intermediary. Bodkin had expected some formality, like being greeted by an introverted, demented assistant, or maybe a tough security guard who spoke few words, with a menacing bulge under his sport coat. Nope. Just Irwin Kagel. A little, fastidious bald guy with thick glasses and tufts of grey hair puffing out above either ear.

The slightly built man gave Bodkin a nod and a handshake, warmer than Bodkin had suspected it would be, then he greeted Sheba with touches to the face and head. Usually Bodkin liked to do the introducing between new people and the dog, as Sheba maintained a jumpy persona and didn't like strangers as a rule. But Kagel had initiated his contact immediately and smoothly, and Sheba didn't seem to mind, showing no feelings of intrusion. This little guy had a way with animals, no doubt.

Hmm. Good sign, Bodkin had thought upon seeing this. Nothing that followed during the visit had contradicted that early impression.

Then Kagel signaled them to follow, waving one arm to come hither, the brilliant Florida sun shining off his white lab coat. White coat: for show, playing the wise doctor? Somehow Bodkin didn't think so. Something told Bodkin this non-threatening man might live fully in the world of research and science. A white lab coat might be second nature to him, almost part of him in essence. Bodkin noticed an absence of pretense. Unlike the medical and pre-med students at the university long ago, during Bodkin's year and a quarter attending classes at Minnesota. They often wore their lab coats, with stethoscopes intact, around their necks everywhere, even while going to lunch. Gotta keep that status on display, Bodkin had figured. In any case, Kagel certainly appeared to be the real deal, status or no.

Small talk and smiles ensued, then Bodkin and his attack dog followed Irwin Kagel into the compound. The two men and the wolf-dog stayed in the very front section of the building; as it turned out, there was to be no walk-through of the rest of the compound in any way.

"Veterinary medicine procedures are done in this section of the facility," Kagel said to Bodkin, a pleasant smile in place. "This is our pet clinic. From here on back, the compound is restricted from the public, for research purposes. We keep it inaccessible to anyone other than staff."

And, true to Kagel's word, the rest of the building definitely appeared to be sealed off. Any passage from the pet clinic to the further reaches of the compound was blocked by two massive, stainless steel doors. The doors featured built-in locks, which if described as "heavy duty" would signify the understatement of the century. Bodkin was an old hand, a semi-expert really, at picking locks. Those locks – three of them – suggested impenetrability the moment he had viewed them. No matter to Bodkin; he just wanted Sheba to receive treatment. He had no real interest regarding what lay beyond those heavy doors. But, that said, he was a little curious.

Bodkin thought back to the facility's strangeness, and especially to one aspect: a presence that seemed as though it floated about the place, regardless of the comforting setting of the pet hospital section of the compound.

The strange presence was basically some kind of dank, musty smell that swished by off and on, as if wisps escaped through the cracks of the door, and maybe from underneath it as well. Otherwise the facility was odorless, no doubt due to the whisper-quiet, cutting edge ventilation system that hummed gently on occasion. Sheba smelled something too, as she kept peering toward the base of the doors. But she didn't seem to register a threat. Just interest, as if she was about to meet another dog. A harmless, friendly one. Or something.

So Bodkin asked Kagel some related questions, not caring too much about the answers. Irwin Kagel, conversely, seemed to care quite a bit about the privacy of the information at hand.

"So, Dr. Kagel, any other life forms behind those heavily reinforced doors there?" Bodkin had asked. "For your research?"

"Like living animals?" Kagel said.

"Pretty much that, yeah," Bodkin said. As opposed to?

"Of course, in terms of being alive. But what remains alive back there is certainly not for experiments. We've got other candidates for hands-on research."

Bodkin waited.

"Some others are in suspended animation, you could say. Living, technically, but not really alive. Specimens who won't feel anything," Kagel said.

"Brain dead?" Bodkin said.

"Yes, that's a lay person's way to put it."

"Those are for experimental purposes, then."

"Yep," Kagel replied.

"What kind of animals?" Bodkin said.

"Tell you what. If you're ever hired as part of this facility's team I'd be glad to give you the complete rundown," Kagel said. "Plus a tour." Kagel smiled then, and not a fake smile. The doctor could disarm, no question. Probably how he managed to live in the same town as the cops here, Bodkin figured.

"I imagine getting onto the staff at a place like this would take tons of experience," Bodkin said.

"Yes, that, and the wait is longer than many are willing to endure. Just for the paperwork, no less," Kagel said. "You've worked for the Feds. You know about their delays."

"Oh yeah. Just trying to get a lunch voucher while out in D.C. has been challenge enough," Bodkin said. "So this is a federal government facility, then?"

A moment of silence followed.

"This was quite the bite, wasn't it?" the doctor said, changing the subject while examining Sheba's wound.

"Certainly. Any idea what that beast was, Dr. Kagel?"

"Why venture a guess? You're the tracker. The talk in town is the cops want you to contract with them on the chase. If you take up the track, I'm sure you'll get up close and personal," Kagel said. "You'll be able to see the subject in detail. And vanquish it. Then I can take over."

"Take over with what?"

"The research. Dissection, autopsy, analysis. You know."

"Seems like you don't foresee whatever that is out there being captured alive," Bodkin said.

"That's correct. Earth's most brutal rarely submit to captivity," Kagel said.

It seemed to Bodkin that the doctor knew a little more than he had let on…but, that's how things go. Bodkin pressed no further.

"I encourage you to help the police here," Kagel said. "Accept the assignment. People are getting killed."

"I'll take it under advisement," Bodkin had said. He'd then waited, figuring Kagel would elaborate. But the doctor didn't. Instead, a sheepish look had come over Kagel's face, and he went on with treating Sheba.

As he thought back on the day's events, Bodkin shifted his head from its position on the wall, adjusting parts of his body to let the beat up areas experience their impending inflammation from different angles. Spread around the misery, basically. As Bodkin did so, the budget bed frame creaked in protest. The levels of pain migrated around in his neck, back, and shoulders, as Bodkin replayed the moment when Irwin Kagel got down to business with Sheba. Specifically, when he warned that it was time to administer the local anesthetic shots, and asked that Bodkin please secure his animal while it happened.

He accordingly secured Sheba, instructed her to keep cool, and Kagel went ahead with the shots. Quick, expert, gentle; the needle stuck into two spots near the wound, then done. Sheba showed no signs of pain, suggesting she barely knew anything with penetrating needles had transpired at all. Dr. Irwin Kagel had a way, Bodkin could see that much.

Bodkin stroked Sheba's face and neck while Kagel's soft, capable hands worked over her light-colored coat, removing specks of blood with disinfectant wipes. Then the doctor picked with care and discarded the dark hairs left near the wound by the attacker, using both wipes and sanitized tweezers, setting the fur specks amongst the little pile of spent wipes. The small cluster of the assailant's hairs accumulated on the wipes, forming a sinister bristle of fur, a strange type of stiff fur coming from an unknown type of beast. Bodkin appreciated the detail-oriented doctor's cleaning of that alien shit from his precious dog's wound.

Stitch, stitch, small talk, stitch, soothing talk from veterinarian to animal, more stitching.

Done. So brief. Bodkin was impressed.

Off they went, dog and master. Back to the motel, for food and rest. No fish fillets yet of course, thanks to that freak attacker thing. So again to the House of Zheng. This time two separate orders of beef and broccoli: one non-spiced, one "China Spicy," as the menu referred to it. Which with the help of plenty of chili peppers, it certainly was. With his tongue burning and sinuses clearing, Bodkin dumped the entirety of the second beef concoction in Sheba's dish, save for the extra rice. He needed the additional glucose boost himself, and devoured the rice mixed in with his China Spicy heap. Sheba preferred the meat feast anyway. Typical ravenous wolf-dog. Bodkin whirled a little square from his plate's beef supply toward the dog, and Sheba snatched it between hungry teeth before it hit the floor. There, that evened up things.

The dog ate quickly, Bodkin ate slowly, and as she keeled over on the linoleum floor to sleep, Bodkin let his mind wander.

He'd been in nicer motel rooms, but worse ones as well. In a small and partially forgotten town like Chicola, it wasn't easy to gather up the money to build the Taj Mahal. At least the floor Sheba was sleeping on was spotless. Didn't want any contaminants getting into the stitched up wound area on the dog's back. Bodkin's eyes traveled along the clean vinyl floor as he daydreamed. He remained motionless, still sleep-deprived, pissed off about being bested, more or less, by some kind of ape-thing freakazoid. Then he noticed something, down on the floor.

Not a perfectly clean floor, upon closer inspection. Some remnants of material, or maybe dark thread or lint it looked like, had been scattered near the door. The light was dim inside the room; Bodkin got up and flicked on the lamp on the room's tiny desk. He walked toward the debris to examine it.

Not thread or lint…no, it was hair. A few specks of hair. Specifically, strands of fur. Same stuff, as far he could tell, as Dr. Kagel had been removing from Sheba's coat and wound. Kagel was precise and exacting in his methods; Bodkin was sure that no fur remnants, virtually none, had been left on Sheba's body. He counted eight little fur strands on the floor.

Why were there strands of that fur in this room?

Had someone tracked something in here? Bodkin looked over to the area close to the bed, then toward the kitchen area, then near the bathroom. No fur strands anywhere else. Only by the door.

Where he himself had stepped, before removing his boots. He bent over and scooped up one of his hunting boots.

In the tread of the boots, sure enough, several more of the fur strands had embedded themselves. So Bodkin himself had tracked in the hairs. Thus the specks of fur lying near the door, but not in the rest of the room. As usual, Bodkin had removed his footwear before entering. He set the boot back down.

During the struggle with that wild freak, some of its filthy fur must have come underfoot, as man, dog, and beast scrambled and battled. One or both boots stomped down in the fighting area, and thus the fur strands got imprinted along with the mud, and were now riding along.

He felt suddenly unclean due to the fur's presence. Bodkin was about to look for a broom somewhere in the motel room's two closets; clean the room, then go dip the boots in some ocean water or something. Then he stopped.

Whoops. Earth to Bodkin. He had to snap out of it. What had he been thinking? Although, granted, a number of factors could have contributed to his failure to piece things together in this case. The lack of sleep, the quickly unfolding chain of events, the entire experience so different from what Bodkin imagined before arriving. Getting clubbed in the face by a monster's fist may have contributed as well.

But no matter. He thought Kagel's laboratory setting was strange before, but the new realization stepped the weirdness of the place up a couple of rungs.

Bodkin now looked over at his fishing shoes by the door. Those shoes, the ones he'd been wearing when navigating the creek. The ones he'd had on when the beast thing attacked.

The hunting boots with the hairs squashed into the tread? At the time of the attack at the creek, they'd been locked up, resting on the floor in the back of his truck. The only place he'd worn them while in town was from the motel to the police station, and soon after to Irwin Kagel's compound.

As Dr. Kagel had removed the hairs from the dog, he had done so with purpose. The attacker's hairs in Sheba's coat clung there, and the ones in the wound stayed even more embedded. Maintaining enough cling that they had to be picked out with tweezers.

So the mysterious fur strands certainly hadn't been drifting off Sheba, at the lab or before, especially not at the rate that Bodkin would have more than a dozen pressed into the underside of his boots. Only one thing to conclude from the scenario.

Before he and Sheba had ever visited the place, the strands of fur had already been on the floor of Irwin Kagel's compound.

13

Coarse black hairs, from a beast not quite like anything that had ever before existed on earth, drifted from the reaches of the massive cypress tree to the marsh water below. The alligator near which the fur landed never noticed it.

The reptile was focusing on dead and dying fish in the swamp. In this case the fish were juveniles from the local population of black acara, a specimen similar to the mainland's freshwater sunfish. The highly prolific and relatively small acara had a seasonal die-off every autumn, as food sources dwindled, swamp levels receded, and the water became less oxygenated. And every year, scavengers like herons, turtles, and of course alligators closed in to partake of the easy bounty.

The creature knew this, and had come here to capitalize on the opportunity. It now waited for the alligator to crawl directly under its own position in the tree. Still too far back for the creature to drop down upon it, the alligator opened its mouth slightly, let another limp acara carcass swish into it, clamped it shut and swallowed the tiny dead prey. Its eyes then examined the swamp water surface for more floating fish bodies.

The creature had earlier trembled with rage as it waited in the tree, but was now in a motionless state. It positioned itself in attack mode on the bulky cypress branch, just over a swampy inlet. It sat 13 feet above the water; the swamp was only two feet deep directly below. Quite shallow, but plunging down would hardly be risky to the creature's safety; soft mud resting on the swamp's bottom would provide cushioning. No matter, in any case: the creature didn't worry about that portion of the ambush. It had done it before with no problem. Besides, the plan was to let the reptile below take the brunt of the impact when the creature slammed down onto it.

Just another few feet, and the alligator would be in perfect position. The creature was here to hunt alternative prey, but had initially climbed into the tree branches earlier to rest and sulk, fuming about its thwarted hunting attempt that morning. Thwarted and ruined when the combative human and that skinny dog crossed its path. They'd interfered with its plan, and both had thus earned a special place on its psychological kill list. It had the capacity to remember, and it wouldn't forget their appearance. Especially not that irreverent human, the one who liked to fight back. The creature wasn't used to humans returning its aggression.

That one was just the kind of arrogant little human glob the creature had been groomed to destroy. Groomed during those years when the creature was cared for…accepted by its trainers. Part of the group. Then it finally chose to lead the group, which in its mind was inevitable. That's when the groomers turned on him, rejected him. Shunned him. It brought the creature anger, and something like sadness, although that concept was still beyond its grasp. Every day since declaring its independence it felt misery in general.

Well, the creature had been making up for it in the past few months, that was certain. How many disgusting human victims had it vanquished so far? Not enough, the creature was positive on that count.

And the dog? Ferocious, but not in the way the creature saw itself to be. The dog didn't seem like a danger to the creature, at least not if the canine was to fight alone. In earlier training – also performed by its disloyal former teachers – personal defense routines had been initiated and drilled. Defense against humans, sure, but also against a thing the trainers had referred to as a "leopard." The creature remembered that they'd used that sound to describe the images. And it had been trained for fending off others, like "hyenas," much closer to the dog physically than the big cats had been. In comparison, the dog was less frightening.

The creature had never actually been in the presence of a leopard or hyena. Instead, the trainers had it view life-size screens, up close, showing the predators' maneuvers. Then wrestling and throwing dummies, designed in the shape of the predators, had served as the objects that the creature could pound on and bite into after viewing. Nothing nearly as fulfilling as vanquishing real animals and humans, but it had been a great outlet and practice method for the creature.

Back to real life. The creature now watched the reptile as it moved forward in the shallow water, waiting calmly for more little dead fish to appear. The creature had switched its own emotional state, as best it could, to one of infinite patience to match the alligator's calm. Stillness was a requirement for most ambushes. A rage state would have to wait. And the waiting would make its fitful rage all that much sweeter, once it was possible to unleash it.

The creature would now take the spirit of the attack beyond movie screens and throwing dummies. Way beyond. The alligator below was fully the creature's own length, and even in the most delusional state of arrogance, any life form could sense in its primal brain that the alligator and its jaws were not to be trifled with. Thus the creature's choice to use its favorite ambush method. Death from above.

The alligator swished forward, eyeing another nearly dead fish. Its jaws had just opened, with the water and little fish starting to circulate into its maw, when an explosion like bursting dynamite ignited its senses.

The alligator was lifted clear of the swamp's surface, its thrashing body held in place from behind by the creature, a constricting squeeze by massive arms trapping it as the creature's fangs crunched into place at the base of the reptile's head.

Two seconds later, the reptile was heaved out of the swamp and onto land, reducing the advantage water would give it. Then slammed belly-first down into the dirt, the creature still astride its back, a vice grip still locked in place around the reptilian throat.

An arch back by the creature to pressurize the reptile's spine, a tighter lockdown on the strangle hold around its neck, and another deep bite into its head was enough to immobilize the alligator. The creature held this position for several more seconds, the alligator now scarcely able to move a muscle.

Then the creature arose, releasing its hold on the prey's neck, and the alligator attempted to follow the creature's position. But the reptile's primitive reflexes had been dulled, most of its strength now sapped, its skull pierced, its system thrust into shock. The creature rose to a crouch and clutched the alligator by the end of its tail.

Whisked through the air in a semi-circle, the alligator could but flail its short legs in futile motions. Then its snout smacked into the trunk of the nearest cypress tree, the one from which the creature had dropped. The reptile was launched in the other direction next and slammed to the ground, its body bouncing back up a few inches with the tremendous force. Another semi-circle, the impact into the cypress trunk this time at the side of its skull. Then pounded to the muddy ground again.

Acute rage ignited inside the creature's brain as it performed the assault. Rage. Pain. Despair. Exhilaration. Joy.

Thump. Slam. Thump. Slam. Picturing its enemies, the humans, with each impact. And none of them more so than the man-thing from this morning, the human glob who dared to fight back. The one with the skinny blonde dog, the one who would be dead except for the help of that slender canine.

Rage!

One final slam of the alligator into the earth, and the creature stopped its onslaught. After looking down at the lifeless body of the alligator for a moment, it paused, its breath now heaving. Rest was desired, although not crucial at this point. This was its second altercation of the day. Pleasing but taxing at the same time. It leaned back against the same tree trunk it had used as an anvil to smash the alligator's brain into useless pulp. It would consume some of the alligator, especially its brain matter, but not yet. Rest, let the breathing even out, let the heat of battle dissipate.

As it did, the creature pictured the adversaries from this morning. The creature would soon pulverize that combative little human weakling, beat him worse than it had the reptile now at its feet.

The man-thing, that disrespectful human glob, was the new target. He would not survive long, nor would that dog that ran with him.

14

Terrence Powell stepped up to the car rental counter.
The Tallahassee Airport at this time in the evening
seemed slow and calm. Or maybe it was always sparsely
populated, for all Powell knew. Perhaps people from
around the country and the world came here seldom, and
the concourse was always partly abandoned. As to what
these warm-weather rubes down here did on a daily basis
and why they did it: who cared? Powell surely didn't.

"Help you, sir?" said the young man behind the
counter, his green and white uniform looking freshly
ironed and crisp. He wore a matching expression, eager
to help.

Powell looked at the rep behind the counter with
slight amusement, said nothing, and handed him a
printout of his reservation.

"OK, very well, sir," the young man said, examining
the sheet and clacking the keyboard accordingly. "So we
have a four-door compact reserved for one week, with—"

"I don't know what they booked for me," Powell
interrupted. "But I need an all-wheel drive, not a
compact." Powell looked at the customer service rep,
suggesting the young man in the green and white outfit
should have known that already.

"OK, one moment. Let's see if we can find
something for you," the rep said, further clacking the
keyboard. The young man's eagerness was fading a little.

As he waited for the customer service rep to
determine the rental options, Powell further surveyed the
other travelers in the airport concourse. A bunch of
dopey looking guys wandered about, not anyone up to

his level of sophistication to be sure. A woman here and there, but Powell didn't see much to look at. According to his standards, that is. Not much different than small town Wyoming. The average could be of even lesser quality here. Then he saw...her.

Bouncing along, standing out from the drab world around her, bright blonde hair fastened back in a simple ponytail. Small in height but tall in stature. Broken-in jeans, broken-in cowboy boots, a shiny, long-sleeved silver top stretched tight across her upper body. Probably silk. In the crook of her arm she cradled a black leather jacket.

He watched the little blonde gal as she walked, displaying energy and confidence, but somehow fatigue as well. There was a subtle move to her hips, sexy, but like an athlete, not a bar fly. Former gymnast or soccer player maybe. Was this how they grow them in Florida? Maybe not so bad here after all, Powell considered.

Ah, to not be so busy all the time. Rushing hither and yon, fulfilling this obligation and that, befriending extraterrestrials and land monsters. On and on. He watched the small, trim blonde moving along, her motions so purposeful yet elegant.

If he was ever to see that one again, in a more relaxed setting, he'd know what to do. Strike up conversation, start off by impressing. Drop a few credentials, mention some influential contacts he had. Maybe even mention his toys, the Land Rover and the Jaguar. The Land Rover was technically the institute's, but the ladies didn't need to know that. Plus one other thing, a very nice thing, as far as Powell was concerned.

Word of the Florida killings had excited a couple of his benefactors in the Bureau of Land Management; they really wanted him, their man, to become the liaison to the Sasquatch. An actual Sasquatch. Their reflective glory, their credit by association, would be immense if Powell connected. They also clearly told him on the conference call that he had an open checkbook for this project. That generous budget could be used for, among other things, wining and dining a client, right? She wouldn't be a client, in actuality, but Powell knew he could make up something if questioned about it by the bigwigs.

The young man looked back up at Powell. Powell reluctantly stopped watching the petite woman in jeans and cowboy boots.

"We do have a Volvo XC90 in all-wheel drive."

"Fine," Powell said.

"I'm sure that will fit your needs," the young man said.

"It better," Powell said. The rep looked at Powell for a moment. His eagerness had now disappeared.

"And I should mention, that is in our top-tier rental price category. That still OK?" the young man said.

"I wouldn't have requested it if I couldn't afford it," Powell said. Actually, the institute could afford it, Powell wouldn't pay a dime of his own money toward anything here…but why bother the flunky in front of him with details?

Powell looked back to the spot he'd last seen the attractive little blonde. Gone. Stupid customer service punk made him lose sight of her. No matter, he would remember the image. He'd wander the concourse a bit and find her. Pretend to be looking for his luggage pickup carousel or something. Fitted jeans, cowboy boots, fluffy blonde ponytail, with a black leather jacket in the crook of her arm.

***

It had been less than a week, and Bodkin realized that he already missed her. Gladdis Montrose wandered across the floor of the Tallahassee Airport toward him now, fatigued and worn, yet purposeful and in control. Beautiful too, although Bodkin resisted thinking about her in those terms.

She wore old, form fitting jeans, cowboy boots, and a stretchy silk top. Pretty much her usual. In the crook of her arm she carried her black leather jacket. The jacket was the minimum for up in Minnesota, but way too much for down here, Bodkin thought. Being equipped for all eventualities was the norm when traveling between climate zones, of course.

"I guess you did lose round one," Gladdis Montrose said, surveying his face with its developing black eye.

"Yeah, no time to get a headgear in place before it nailed me. But I got to demonstrate my bob and weave punch evasion, so there were some pluses," Bodkin said.

"We'll get the thing."

"That's the spirit," Bodkin said.

He extended his arm, fist gently closed for a bump. Montrose brushed it aside and scooped him around the waist, then leaned her head heavily on his chest. Bodkin could feel the usual springy tone of her musculature mixed with a deep exhaustion.

"Plenty of sand, sun, and empty beach awaiting you, girlie. And espresso. Plus the House of Zheng."

"Which is?"

"Our food supply. You'll see," Bodkin said.

"We've got another job to do first," Montrose said.

"Yeah, but we've got Sheba to supervise. And now you. So no problem," Bodkin said.

"The toothsome gal waiting out in the truck?"

"Certainly."

"Awesome," Montrose said. Bodkin scooped the jacket from her, and she traded it for Bodkin's arm, leaning sideways into him, watching the luggage come out onto the carousel. Looking at ease and half asleep at the same time. They stood there, awaiting her impact-resistant suitcase and its specialized contents. Montrose closed her eyes as she leaned her head on his shoulder.

Bodkin saw the guy then for the third time. A prissy academic type, all decked out in clothing of the type from L.L. Bean, Orvis, Timberland, and Marmot. Similar to what he and Montrose wore…but this guy's duds all looked brand new.

The guy was checking out Gladdis. He was making an attempt at being surreptitious, but was no good at it. Bodkin was used to this type of thing when Gladdis was near other men, and didn't really care that much. But this clown was actually on the hunt, looking around a pillar before, then hiding behind some airport signage as he stared. In stalk mode you could say. Bodkin and his partner liked to perform the stalk, not be the object of it.

Bodkin wasn't in the mood. He turned and looked straight at the man. No malice or badass theater, just a steady gaze. The guy glanced at Bodkin, did a double take, then tried to return Bodkin's stare. It lasted four seconds. The guy sniffed, raised his chin up so he was looking at Bodkin down his nose, then turned on the heel of a spendy but rarely used hiking shoe.

Bodkin watched the fussy-looking guy for a moment as he retreated through the expanse of the airport. Then he looked back at the restive face of Gladdis Montrose, nearly asleep on his shoulder. She was actually gentle when she slept; that was one of the rare times. Bodkin let his eyes wander to the carousel. He watched for the luggage while anticipating their long ride in the dark back to Chicola.

15

"I feel like the ice block I've been stuck inside of is starting to melt away already. Lee my boy, I think you were right about the need for me to switch climates for awhile," Gladdis Montrose said.

"Even a broken clock is right twice a day," Lee Bodkin said. He looked straight out from the truck as he spoke, watching the entire parking lot. "But I'll take a round of applause wherever I can get one."

Montrose said nothing. She slouched down in the seat of the truck, feeling the sun creep through the open window, while the two of them continued to watch the front and side of the hotel. Waiting for the vaunted researcher to come out to his rented Volvo.

Last night Bodkin saw Gladdis to her room – over at the Holiday Inn, no Sea Foam Inn for Ms. Montrose. It was not too unusual for them to be apart overnight. They often stayed in separate hotels, to each have their own space, yes, but also for strategic reasons. They'd made many an enemy over the years, arresting or sometimes killing biker gang members, hitmen, and organized crime players. And perhaps worst of all, serial killers. Most of these sociopaths and degenerates had associates and family members left behind who might want vengeance. And that did in fact include the serial killers: the number of scumbag thrill killers who worked in tandem with a partner was pretty chilling once you learned about it.

So staying separate from each other allowed Bodkin and Montrose to present a harder target, and afforded them the chance to come to each others' rescue. It had paid off several times so far over the years. Contact via cell phone as well as by good old walkie talkie was a crucial ingredient in such a situation. The bad guys often assumed that Bodkin and Montrose were lovers and thus stayed together in a given place of lodging. Wrong on both counts, which more than once had resulted in the enemy being taken out without a clue, unaware completely about who was sneaking up from behind in the dark. Sometimes it sucked to be the bad guy.

Once they'd checked in last night at the Holiday Inn and went up to her digs, Gladdis had collapsed on the bed, still in her clothes. Not sleeping, just staring at the ceiling in jittery exhaustion. Bodkin contacted room service and acquired a fat ham and cheddar sandwich for her and a turkey and provolone for himself. Each serving contained a big pile of salty chips on the plate. They feasted immediately, and in the course of things Gladdis forfeited most of her chips to Bodkin. He liked her a little better at that moment. Seeing as he had 400 extra calories worth of chips, Bodkin saved half of the meat on his sandwich for the wolf-dog back in his own room. It worked out perfectly for all involved.

After wrapping the meat in a napkin, he left Gladdis there and headed out for his next stop: the police station, and Sergeant Grady Morton.

Bodkin had planned to call Morton at his home if needed, but as luck had it, Morton was on site. The key to the visit: find out about this enthusiast guy who was coming to town from some institute out west. The one who was reported to be a specialist in unusual life forms, in this case a supposed Sasquatch. A short time ago, Bodkin would have scoffed at the claim of such a creature even existing; now, especially after a brief hand-to-hand battle and a furry fist to the face, Bodkin was hesitant to dismiss any such concept. Sasquatch or whatever, maybe. Big disgusting violent monster with an attitude, definitely.

As Bodkin saw it, he and Gladdis would be starting from square one regarding tracking this hairy being in the swampy brush. Sheba would help immensely of course, the beast's scent serving as her new most hated odor on earth, most likely. But it would be difficult, as well as dangerous. Surprise attacks were a major bummer if you weren't the party carrying them out.

So he decided to forget starting from ground zero, unless no other choice was available. Luckily, it appeared like another option did in fact exist. And the researcher who'd soon be arriving in town would provide it: a shortcut to their objective that Bodkin could capitalize on. An impromptu meeting with the gangly Sergeant Morton was in order.

Why seek out tactics and methods to track down a new threat when you could just hijack a known method for finding it? Thus the focus on this institute researcher guy who'd arrive soon.

The man from the secretive institute would commence his tracking of the monster thing. As he did it, Bodkin and Montrose would then track the researcher. Bada-bing.

After they'd wandered outside the station, Bodkin proceeded to interrogate Morton, gently and diplomatically. Just a conversation really, regarding who the researcher guy was, when he'd arrive, and where he was staying. The slender sergeant was more than willing to share it all, sensing Bodkin kind of liked him. Which he did. And Morton assumed he and Bodkin were now on the same team. Which, Bodkin started to realize, they sort of were. Ooo, boy. This should be…interesting.

"So you're officially taking the assignment?" Morton had asked Bodkin.

"We'll be looking into things, starting tomorrow morning. You can tell the chief," Bodkin said.

"There's more than one of you now?" Morton said.

"Yes. So let the chief know we're starting the tracking process."

"Is it that woman?"

"Uh, yeah, it's 'that woman.' Just a couple of questions before I go, Sergeant Morton," Bodkin said.

"Can I meet her?"

"We'll see. Now…"

"I should mention, if you haven't filled out the application and contract forms, I'm not sure the town council here can guarantee you'll get paid for services rendered," Morton said.

"So it's like that, huh?"

Morton shrugged.

"Well, then I guess we don't get paid, and I go back out on the beach."

"You're a pretty cool cucumber," Morton said. Bodkin thought he might next ask for an autograph.

"Questions," Bodkin said.

"Uh, yeah," Morton said. "Shoot."

Bodkin thus had found out the answers to who, why, when and where. And now, the morning after, he and Montrose sat nearly motionless in his truck, saving their energy. Waiting in the lot of the highest rated hotel in town, the DoubleTree Royale. Watching a rented Volvo SUV that had been parked there, waiting for its operator to show.

They didn't wait long: less than 45 minutes after sunrise, a jaunty, bespectacled man navigated the lot, with chin up and a face sporting both pride and disdain. Bodkin recognized him from the airport – it was the guy who was watching them, or specifically *her*, at the luggage pickup area. Decked out in newer outdoor adventure togs, probably from places like L.L. Bean, Orvis, Timberland, and Marmot. Same as yesterday. The man, one Terrence Powell, popped open the back door of the Volvo, set two gear bags on the seat there, then hopped into the vehicle and pulled out of the lot.

Time to roll.

16

"Got it?" Bodkin said.

"Yep," Montrose replied. She saved the coordinates of the Volvo's location, then lowered the GPS and set it next to her on the seat. Both of them peered off and on into the brush next to the dirt road, anticipating.

They'd just driven past Kagel's compound, maybe a quarter mile back. At this point there were no houses, gas stations, or cafes. Just tall grass, dense, dark forest, and humid marshland. A long way from the Florida Everglades, but this area didn't appear to be much different. Wild and untamed, peaceful and hostile at the same time.

Bodkin continued to drive his truck at a slow pace, away from the position where Terrence Powell had pulled over onto the road's shoulder. Powell was not visible anywhere nearby, but he could be holding still back in the greenery, watching. Bodkin and Montrose maintained their slow drive, eyes ahead as much as possible, as they rolled along. Masquerading as just some local bumpkins driving about, attending to their daily business. Bodkin's faded old pickup truck fit the part.

With the coordinates, they planned to park up ahead, just out of sight, then come back through the dense forest and swampland. They'd pick up Powell's track, follow from a distance, and see what the researcher stumbled upon.

Bodkin selected a roadside spot just around the first bend, only 120 yards from Powell's SUV but completely hidden from that area due to unending foliage.

They exited the truck. Sheba stepped over to where a weedy drainage ditch ran alongside of the road, then looked past that water to the vast marshy morass beyond, surveying the jungle ahead. While the dog picked up new scents and got into the groove, Montrose opened a duffle bag in the back seat and withdrew the warm-weather camouflage she'd brought along from home.

After handing Bodkin his top, she put on her own over a sleeveless running shirt. The camo garment consisted of a thin polyester mesh, with the fabric woven with countless "pores" to let heat escape and cooling breeze blow in. A porous yet amazingly tough construction made the camo suitable for hunting amongst and up against jagged tree bark, sharp sticks, and prickly thorns. The olive hunting pants on her lower body, with all 17 pockets, had seen even more duress in forest and field.

Bodkin stretched his own camouflaged shirt over a beat up Minnesota Vikings tee, then took the grey tree branch pattern bandana she handed him. He whirled it around his head and knotted it in back like a businessman finessing a silk tie. It went swimmingly with his dull khaki Carhartt work jeans and mud-colored hunting boots. Montrose whipped together her own bandana headdress, ensconcing and hiding the handfuls of bright blonde hair that rested there.

Now outfitted, Bodkin and Montrose looked like a pile of decaying leaves mixed with dead brush. The woodland stalker's ideal.

Montrose removed her rifle from the truck floor, behind where she'd sat. An extra blanket from Bodkin's motel room had been draped over the weapon in blousy fashion. Hidden as such it would attract less attention, both while exiting the Holiday Inn and as it rested in

Bodkin's truck. As Bodkin watched Montrose glide a magazine full of high power bullets into the rifle's underside – soundlessly, not with a slam like in the movies – he thought of how smooth his partner was, and how they were transitioning into their usual hunter roles so effortlessly. All old hat for both of them, performed a thousand times. But at this time he was supposed to be on vacation, just he and Sheba. And now this, out of the blue. He didn't regret it, and was more amused than anything. Down here in Florida, a place where they'd never done a job, but transitioning without a hitch, doing their thing regardless. The process, this morning before sunrise, was a perfect example.

Bodkin had been lying awake, five hours of sleep plus a short nap refreshing him. Not enough, but you have to rise to the occasion, as he knew all too well. He'd been wondering how Gladdis would fare today, if at all. Bodkin was worn down, but no insomnia victim was he, ever. Gladdis, on the other hand, occasionally was. Maybe because she had a conscience? If that was so, what did it say about Bodkin, if he could kill then go right back to sleep? He decided to forget that for the moment. Anyway…

He was pondering how soon he should go over to the Holiday Inn and rouse her from the room. Just as he decided the time was now, the knock at the door came. Well, well. No scrambling for a weapon, no whispering to find out who was there. Three short raps on the door, around its center, then two soft ones high on the door, near the top. Sheba had arisen, and swished her tail slowly back and forth at hearing the sound. The dog recognized their agreed-upon knock sequence, one the two bounty hunters had used for years. Code for Gladdis Montrose has arrived.

Montrose certainly looked more refreshed than she had the previous night. Ready for action, no less. Bodkin would quiz her about her night's sleep later.

After Bodkin readied himself in a calm scramble, they went back to her hotel and up to the room: armament time. As Bodkin waited and relaxed, from her suitcase Montrose withdrew the components that had been secured there, presented in a way as to not reveal the true nature of what the gadgets were to be used as.

Some of the sections had been disguised as a camera tripod, others were set into the structure of the luggage itself, helped by the suitcase being equipped with a false bottom. The components' weight was negligible, so mass wasn't much of an issue. Padding hid the shape of the sections. And those parts were enshrouded with a special plastic alloy that prevented detection on TSA viewers at the airport. Not the kind of gear you got at Home Depot.

In seven minutes, Montrose had assembled the biathlete rifle, which was a duplicate of the one she used in competition. This gun, as opposed to her tournament rifle, fired higher power ammunition. It shot wicked, slender bullets in .243 caliber, which when placed appropriately would kill a full-grown deer. She'd used the same design of bullets to do just that in the past, many times. This particular rifle had killed a handful of big game animals for the freezer, as well as a few bad guys and one very bad woman.

Montrose removed two rifle magazines from the suitcase next, each also housed in a sheath of the concealing plastic alloy. She removed the sheaths from both magazines, set those plastic housings carefully back into the suitcase for future use, and placed the bullet clips into the leg pockets of her hunting trousers. Montrose next handed Bodkin two little round devices with cartridges protruding out one side, the items looking like miniature wagon wheels. The shells they contained were .357 magnum bullets for his handgun.

"I realistically could only fit a dozen of 'em," Montrose said. "Hope that will hold you over."

"Should be good. We'll see. But I gotta say, sure feel like I could use another 50 shots as backup after the scrape with that thing," Bodkin said.

"I brought along 18 rounds for myself, guy. We're good," Montrose said.

"Let's hope so."

His comment gave her pause. "It's just a matter of finding the critter, right? Then blasting it?"

Bodkin didn't answer, thinking instead of responding.

"Once we get it trapped or treed or what have you, it's all over for it. Correct?" Montrose said.

"We'll see," Bodkin said.

"This is just one beast, right?" Montrose said. "C'mon Lee, my man, I'm gonna start to think you're slipping. Plus, we've got Sheba, remember?"

"Gladdis," Bodkin said, no playfulness in his voice now. "If this bastard behaves anything like last time, Sheba will only be supplemental to our efforts."

"You don't think she could take whatever it is by herself?" Montrose said. "That is, if it didn't run away like last time."

"I highly doubt it."

Montrose looked a little disappointed. "How about against you? If it stood its ground and took its medicine, I mean."

"I would wager that help would be needed," Bodkin said.

"If you had a knife?"

"I think I'll stick to a large-caliber handgun, thanks. Plus your knack for hitting the bullseye as my backup," Bodkin said. He thought he'd made it pretty clear on the phone how formidable this thing seemed to be.

Montrose was starting to think Bodkin was the more exhausted of the two of them. She just wanted to finish this locating and killing of a rogue animal, then get to the beach to eat, sunbathe, and rest.

"OK, well, don't worry. I'll make sure to shoot straight. Seeing as you're certain this animal or whatever is the ultimate menace."

A specimen such as the creature would have been hard for most anyone to describe, and without seeing it, she'd thrown out the descriptor *ultimate menace*. But at that point, to Gladdis Montrose it was just a concept. Like a wild boar, or a Rottweiler, or a black bear. They could all be menaces, but usually not the ultimate. But for this creature, a special category would have to be created to fully notate its unique propensity for violence, for the level of danger in pursuing it.

And it would not be long until Montrose would see for herself that the description she'd come up with was pretty accurate.

17

Irwin Kagel slammed down the phone. He had to catch his breath for a moment. The incompetent town cops should have let him know earlier. The simplest courtesy would have been to inform him, Irwin Kagel, as a prominent part of the community's leadership. He wasn't on any city council or anything, but for crying out loud. Or was he really still an outsider here in Chicola? Still not one of them? If not, tough shit. People were being killed.

He silently apologized to himself for using profanity, even if it had been in his own mind. Swearing was not his thing. On the other hand...

Fuck!

If that pretend researcher, this Powell character, was actually out there now, as the cops surmised, he was dead meat. Kagel knew the type of guys who worked as extraterrestrial liaisons. They were often part of the Berkeley/Jackson Hole/Boulder set, big on things like grants from government as well as corporate foundations, cocktail parties with other heavy hitters, and BMW SUVs – organization-sponsored of course. They usually bragged about everything they did, or could claim that they had done. Actual communication with any extraterrestrials was always dubious. Photos and audio tracks could be easily altered nowadays. If no one else had been there to prove you didn't interact with an alien life form, you could boast to your heart's content.

This situation here, however, would not be one to boast about. Kagel felt faint even picturing it. If Powell went into the lair, into the belly of the beast, there'd be no discussing it later at a party. Powell venturing out into the wetlands here would be like throwing a wriggling worm into a stream with piranhas. Another dead body, namely Terrence Powell's, was a near certainty.

And it would be on Irwin Kagel. The road to hell was paved with the best of intentions, and intentions had been the only real stuff Kagel had generated without a snafu. And that was to put it mildly...since his best intentions kept getting things killed off and people murdered.

All because of his sincere efforts, his plans, his strategic breeding and training program. Meant to save lives, not destroy them. So many wonderful improvements had been envisioned by his colleague and him. But not a single improvement had materialized, and not a single species had been saved. And his colleague, his partner in brainstorming, was now dead.

If something wasn't done soon, more people would die. Terrence Powell was most likely next.

Because he was about to meet Tuma.

Tuma's face...and fists, and teeth, would be the last thing this Powell guy, this interloper, would ever see.

The cops said Powell was some kind of Bigfoot hunter. What the fuck? Bigfoot? That's what this had evolved into? Heavens. Tuma would have a Sasquatch beaten down and its skull punctured in one minute flat.

Oh God. Kagel, a man of science, of life, wanted to scream. No matter what this Powell fellow did, he would not be received in peace. There would be no understanding, no mercy, no quarter. It was how Tuma had been trained. And that Kagel knew plenty about...he'd directed the training.

Why hadn't he been more assertive with that Bodkin guy, the tracker for hire? *I encourage you to help the police. Accept the assignment.*

That's all he could come up with to convince Bodkin? After his lame statements, Kagel remembered he was at a loss for words for what to say next. Didn't want to reveal too much. So he had said in essence almost nothing to Bodkin that was meaningful. Nothing that painted a true picture of the urgency here.

Irwin Kagel had no way to contact this Terrence Powell man. He didn't know him, had no cell phone number, no information on the researcher at all, other than a name. Neither did the police here in town, not even the man's home office contact information.

And Powell was going out to Tuma's stomping grounds. And right into Tuma's clutches.

18

This should be fun.

That's what Terrence Powell thought, at least at first.

It had been so easy to pick up the data on his life form monitor. He'd went to the police station last night to run a few questions by them, primarily regarding where the recent attacks had occurred. The officers gave Powell a ballpark idea of the general vicinity. Basically that's all he needed for a starting point.

The cops in turn tried to counter with an equal number of inquiries, mainly focused on what Powell's objectives were and what would happen if he succeeded.

No fool was Powell, however. The information regarding his adventure was on a need-to-know basis, and these flunkies didn't need to know any of it. Powell maneuvered around their questions with his artful dodge techniques, in which he considered himself a master. Return their questions with questions of his own as a main strategy. Evasive half answers were another nice tactic. And if backed into a corner, simply invoke his connections with the Department of the Interior, and the requirement of secrecy that came with that association. Powell more or less made that last part up as he went. But they'd bought it, the bozos.

Ah, those cops. The chief was an old macho bloke posing as some kind of cowboy throwback. He'd struck Powell as maybe a former strong man now wishing for those early days, and one determined to show that he still had it at 60 or thereabouts. There was also a slender cop present, kind of a nerd it appeared, in his early 30s maybe, who stood in the background and didn't say much. Name of Morland or Morton or something.

Then there was Officer Slick, a dude named Kevin Kort. Ha, what a peach. A real slickster wannabe with razor cut hair combed straight back. They had security guys like him at the institute in Wyoming, men who mostly drove around in departmental trucks to watch the property and so on, then help with cutting grass and shoveling snow. Once the snow had fallen, those same guys would head to the local ski lodges after work. There they'd try to hit on the lady tourists who'd come into town every winter. Powell had overheard a couple of the security guys saying they were from a special police task force of some kind, leaving out mention of their snow shoveling duties. Nice.

The whole time the chief had questioned Powell, the cop named Kort had kept his head tilted to one side with a little sneer on his face, watching Powell's every move. He'd also kept his chin up and peered at Powell down his nose. Powell especially didn't like that, as the same gesture was one of his own patented moves to establish dominance.

He did, however, like the look of that Kort guy's polished teeth. Maybe when this was over, he'd ask Kort where he'd had it done.

So here he was, in the swamp, now a couple of hundred yards from the SUV, at least. Massive cypress trees towered overhead, ferns and tall grasses choking the ground most places near the giant trunks. Dense and humid, so unlike the Wyoming, Montana, and Idaho mountains. Powell looked back down at the life form monitor. The device was about the same size as a standard size iPad, but two inches thicker or so. He'd have feared being hopelessly lost in the marsh except for the technology he carried. The GPS device inside the life

form monitor would guide him back to the vehicle
without a doubt. It was a flawless mechanism and had
been with him on many expeditions before this. His only
concern was that the muggy air in the region might cause
unforeseen malfunctions. Time would tell.

The life form monitor would help Powell find his
way back, granted, but it did far more than act as a GPS.
He wouldn't currently be in proximity to the animal – it
being a Sasquatch hopefully – without the monitor. The
only way a person could better detect the presence of
such a mysterious beast would be to have a tracking
device literally attached to the thing, then use the device's
receiver to determine a location. Other than that, the life
form monitor was the best tool in the world for it.

The monitor stored selections of the DNA of certain
living beings inside it; those selections could be clicked
off a menu, and the monitor could then be activated to
search them out. In a way not too differently than a
metal detector is used to seek out coins on a beach. You
just had to choose the DNA types, hit Load, then Seek.
And the monitor would start to search for the presence
of such DNA, up to 125 meters out or so.

DNA sources of a Sasquatch? No such thing, not
definitively at least. So the institute had improvised. A
certain type of fur had been found in both California's
Sierra Nevadas and Washington's Cascade mountains,
fur that was hypothesized to be from Sasquatch
specimens. Nothing else could explain the discovered
fur; it matched no hairs from any other living thing.

To provide the closest match to said fur, the
Enlighten Institute selected the fur and skin
characteristics of four organisms: black bear, gorilla,
baboon, and human. The institute concluded those
particular living things came the closest to the physical
origins of the mystery fur. In terms of DNA, and also in

a behavioral sense: the selected creatures were all omnivores, all with similar incisors, all with eyes facing straight ahead, and all able to stand on back legs like a Sasquatch had been reported to do. Using those four DNA profiles was the closest they could get while not straying too far from the molecular structure of the hair they'd found.

Over the years, all of these DNA types and many others had been entered into the brain center of the life form monitor by digitized profile. Each fur type had been evaluated and then scanned into the device's database. Handy. In the field, no actual hair or skin remnants needed to be present, none had to be inserted into or read by the monitor in any way. The database instead stored each DNA profile; the user just selected and clicked. Then the life form monitor started to seek the DNA information that it had been told to find. The user just waited for it to tick and display little red flashes on its screen.

Today, the monitor had started to issue its tick sounds as Powell cruised slowly along the road, around the area the police had told him attacks had occurred. Once the ticks start to really fire, at a few pops a second, Powell knew he was in the right area. He'd started his search from that spot, and as he'd trudged, ticks had steadily emitted from the life form monitor, although sporadically.

Meaning the beast was close, but not close enough.

Powell felt a tingle of excitement at the possibilities here in the Florida marshland; amazed at this chance actually coming to life for him. But, of course…he didn't see a Sasquatch until he actually saw one. Can't get too excited. Let things unfold and play it by ear. Maybe the thing had vacated the area already. If so, he'd better start working on his tall tales as soon as possible. If he could get ahold of that little redneck guy that snapped the photos of the beast, he'd talk the dip out of the pics for a small fee. If the hick wouldn't go along with it, Powell would threaten him with government authority. Terrence Powell had little authority, but the clueless bumpkin wouldn't know that.

Once Powell had the pics, he was set. If he could take none of his own here, those from the bumpkin would become the ones Powell himself had "taken," to go along with a scintillating story he'd devise. So, all in all, this outing had little pressure, providing Powell attained those wild beast action photos.

His thoughts were interrupted by a tick on the life form monitor. Then another. Then a couple of red flashes on the little screen. Then some more. Quickly, and in great number. Powell stopped his plodding through the moist weeds of the wetland, and held still.

Something was approaching. Powell almost told himself something was "closing in," but restrained such thoughts immediately. "Approaching" sounded much more cooperative, much friendlier. Much safer.

Powell looked back at the life form monitor. The flashes on the rectangular screen would show in relation to which direction the targeted living presence was located, based on where the user stood. If something was crouching in the brush behind you, the flashes would be at the bottom of the screen. If said presence was ahead, flashes at the top; to the right, flashes to the right, accordingly. Gentle ticking sounds would emanate from the device at the same time, to alert the user by sound as well as sight.

At the moment, Powell was watching flashes appear not just to the right, to the left, or to the top of the screen; they burst across the screen in all directions, changing by the second. Something was close by, and it was moving. All around him, it seemed. Then he heard the rustling and thumping.

Grass swished, vines whipped, and branches bent nearby. Powell tried to spot what caused the disturbances, looking about in a semicircle. But nothing in animal or human form could be seen where the noises originated. Just dense greenery with its concealing shadows, clustered brush, and hanging tentacles of thick grape vines. Powell froze, listening and watching.

Then he heard a *huff* sound, like a big, heavy man exhaling with force. It came from behind him...but also from above. Powell turned slowly and looked up.

Nobody there; specifically, no *thing* there, not in mammalian form at least. Just a large cypress tree branch, maybe 11 or 12 feet from the ground, covered in wisps of Spanish moss, with a single vine looped over its wide expanse, the vine flipped over the branch then wandering down toward the muddy ground. Powell started to look away, then noticed something: the vine was swaying. There was no wind here, not even a slight breeze. Yet the grapevine tentacle was swinging gently back and forth.

At the moment he realized this, the ground lurched behind him, from the direction he'd originally been facing. Lurched as if there'd been a collision.

And there had been, between dirt, plants, and a big pair of feet. In a split second, Powell processed it as he looked back that way, adrenaline shooting through his system. Something with feet had thumped down to the ground, something heavy, and the being had landed with a deft touch. Like it was trying to cushion its weight and bulk as it came down from a location above...from the trees.

Powell turned fully, looking straight ahead at first, then down. A dark shape hulked there, fur-covered arms and shoulders flared out in ready position, legs bent to bring the being down to a low crouch. Its eyes stared into his. The shape stayed low for a second, then it rose up, its head reaching the same level as Powell's. It was the same height as he, and half again as wide.

Powell guessed he was now face-to-face with the Sasquatch of his dreams; it appeared similar to what he'd imagined, only much more…intent. Much more predatory.

In the shadows of the cypress swamp, the visual signals burst from the life form monitor's screen, reflecting little red flashes off the creature's eyes. The ticks from the device were coming in a frequency similar to a strobe light, issued in a frenzy. Now not individual ticks, but rather a whir of tiny sounds all run together.

Powell could smell a dank, pungent odor drifting from the beast. Like nothing he'd experienced before. A mixture of wildness, wet wool, swamp moisture…and savagery, somehow. The beast was breathing in slowly, and exhaling in an audible but very controlled rhythm. As if restraining anger, or maybe saving up for a burst of action.

Even as this stare-down happened, amazingly, the main thought in Powell's head was not about danger, or his own self-protection, although it should have been. Instead, the resounding realization came to Powell as he looked into the thing's determined eyes, taking in the wide head, the hefty brow bone, the flat nose. And the four sharp incisors as it opened its mouth. At the institute, they'd guessed a genetic combination of a typical Sasquatch to be something close to black bear, gorilla, baboon, and a human being. Here, up close, the combination looked…correct!

Correct, oh yes. Powell could see that now, as he was just 11 feet from the wild being. There could be success, would be, Powell would see to it. Stay calm, he told himself. Powell knew he could make the connection here. He reached out his hand, and extended his index finger.

"I come in peace," Powell said.

Powell pictured the wild being in front of him doing the same thing, and they'd touch finger tips initially. Thereby establishing that first contact, that first inter-species connection. Powell had seen that in a Spielberg movie long ago, with the featured extraterrestrial in that film extending the olive branch with a fingertip touch. The scenes in the film, and memory of the fingertip contact concept, filled Powell with confidence.

The beast took a step toward Powell, and leaned forward. And in that moment, Powell thought the cooperation might happen. Glee flooded through him. He kept his arm extended, his finger reaching out, looking for some fingertip love.

But no reciprocation came from the intense, furry being in front of Powell. The creature not only kept its arms down, it actually turned them inward, contracting and flexing them. And it crouched another inch closer to the ground. Like the posture a predator would assume just before it pounced. Powell glanced down at the large, thick hands of the creature. The hands were not in fact open and accepting, as Powell had hoped. They were instead flexed into fists.

The fists didn't look ready for gentle fingertip contact, exactly. The eyes burning their focus into those of Powell's looked even less friendly. Powell's blind faith started to wane.

Powell took a step toward the creature; it would be the last voluntary movement of his body, ever.

Impact, impact, one to each side of Powell's head. Didn't hurt, not yet, then as Powell buckled and covered his head, nearly falling over, similar pounding blows to his ribs, one to each side. Those hurt. And knocked the wind out him. Powell started to fall, but was clutched and whirled through the air before he could hit the ground.

In a final moment of agonized consciousness, Powell perceived the sensation as he soared through the air with an experience he'd felt when he was a little boy. His first-ever ride on a Ferris wheel, at the state fair. Terrifying, the flying, the dropping, then the salvation, the swooping motion back up as the wheel twirled through, saving you from smashing to the ground. He sailed now, and it felt similar for that instant. Only in this case, an enormous, immoveable tree trunk awaited him as he whipped through the air, helpless.

A shocking, blinding flash. Then oblivion.

***

The creature caught its breath for an instant, evaluating the dead man's head. It would now sink its fangs in, feast, satisfy its cravings. The kill had been joyous…it'd been too long since the last one. That swamp reptile it had recently destroyed just wasn't the same. But here it had a warm-blooded victim down, soft and vanquished. And best of all, human.

It straddled the freshly murdered body of Terrence Powell, adjusting its position to execute the bite.

***

A cream-colored burst of fur and fangs leapt up and onto the creature's back, looking for a neck bite. The creature flung its arms wildly, wailing, dropped and rolled, and came up swinging, its mouth agape and teeth searching for flesh.

Sheba rushed in again, the creature striking at her, swinging a left at the wolf-dog, then a right, missing the attempts as the dog moved with blinding speed, snapping at its legs. Canine fangs sunk into its hip for an instant, and the screeching creature swept the attacking dog aside and retreated on all fours toward the dense greenery. Another snap at its rump made the creature spin and defend, rising back up on two legs.

As the creature crouched to defend itself, it peered past the dog-thing, noticing sudden movement there. From the thick underbrush came what looked to the creature like a moving pile of rotting vegetation. But running, on two legs. Focusing on the leaf and brush morass, the creature recognized a face – a human face – at the top of the heap. It was the man-thing, the weakling glob, the human that had recently fought with the creature, the one the creature was determined to kill. The man-thing held in one hand the shiny thunder maker, just like last time.

Even covered with the brush and leaves, the man-thing moved faster than the creature could ever achieve running upright. There was no hesitation in the charge, the eyes of the stinking man-thing locked on the creature, at a full speed run, heading right at it. Prior to the man-thing, never in the creature's life had a human run *for* it. Humans ran away, at least when they'd had the chance.

The man-thing closed the distance, then slowed, gripped the weapon with both hands, and pointed it straight at the creature.

The creature, shocked and panicked, scrambled on all fours, away to shelter, as another dog bite pierced its body, now on the lower back, and with a single slam of a fist back to free the dog's jaws, the creature sought its ultimate refuge: upward, into the trees.

The creature went up the nearest cypress tree, the trunk a big fat goliath with dense branches. It scrambled upward until the branches became thin and flimsy. It prepared to jump to a nearby tree, the next cypress even bigger. But first the creature looked down.

The stinking man-thing was following it up the tree, at a speed slower than the creature's ascent, but rapid, far too rapid. Clinging to branches and vines, crouching and leaping to the next branch, catching up to the creature.

The creature quickly considered maneuvering down and killing off the man-thing, that weakling glob of a human, but then it remembered the man's thunder maker. A weapon like the ones the creature had been trained to fear in the early days. The creature couldn't see it carried anywhere on the human, and it wasn't in his hands. The man had it hidden, certainly. Still go for the kill? The creature had to make a snap decision, now.

As it weighed the choice, the creature lowered its head for a second, ready to either descend to the man or leap over to the next tree.

A clump of Spanish moss hanging next to its face exploded, and a penetrating blast sounded from below. The creature recoiled, shocked and confused, and clung tightly to the thickest part of the tree. It glanced down; the human below was closing on him, but the human's thunder maker was not out. The creature then took a look around the tree trunk.

Down on the ground, another pile of leaves and brush was moving. It was going steadily to the right of where the creature hid, in a direction where it would eventually see the creature clearly, with no tree in the way. The entire shape was only half the size of the weakling man-glob now climbing up after it. But the shape was just as quick as the speedy man-thing, as it maneuvered through the tall grass and saplings, slithering between branches instead of pushing them aside. Once the leaf and brush blob was directly to its right, no tree blocking the view, a face appeared atop it…just like it had done on the man-thing blob down below.

It was another human…chasing it. The face was smaller, and appeared to be female. The creature knew it could kill that one even easier than it could the male. If it could just get its hands on…a flicker of motion, a glint of a silver pole or something in the female human's hands. Another thunder maker – one of the long ones.

Pointing straight at it!

As realization of what had exploded the Spanish moss next to its head just moments ago careened through the creature's brain, it leapt for the next tree, airborne for almost two seconds. Another piercing blast from below, then another, the bullets popping another Spanish moss tentacle and severing the vine the creature now grasped. The creature flailed, gripped another vine, and swung to the next giant tree trunk, then scrambled to get behind that tree as a shield.

The creature snuck a glance around the trunk; the man-thing was scrambling back to the ground, and the dog-thing was rushing straight under the tree the creature was in now. The creature looked quickly for the female; it was hard for the creature to focus on the human's shape with all the leaves and weeds that seemed to compose her body. There! The female was sprinting right behind the dog, the long thunder maker poised at the ready in her hands.

The creature realized now that it was fully the prey in this situation. It had a burst of fear rocket through it then like the steam shooting from a boiling tea kettle. An unknown sensation, completely foreign to a being that knew it was the most formidable force on earth. The creature began its retreat, this time extending all of its capabilities to the limit. No stopping to glance back. It leapt, clutched, then leapt again.

Tree, tree, another tree, down to a sloppy marsh section once the big cypress trees ended, a scramble in a blind panic, then back up once the monstrous trees began again. Tree, tree, another tree, stop! It hunkered down then, finding a perfect concave in that last tree's column. It was now 19 feet from the ground, and halfway inside the center of a cypress tree's trunk, its own little cave in which to conceal itself.

The creature held still, listening but hearing little. It couldn't bring itself to even look down or around the tree. It faced inward, hunched over, terrified. Like the classic and vicious schoolyard bully, ready for the fight, but only when the odds were ideal. Now it was more like the chastised child, a frightened one. It waited. For hours. It slept there, awoke, then waited some more.

Nightfall came, and all sounds of the stinking humans and the stinking dog were long gone. The regular noise of the nighttime swamp came alive, with all its assorted beasts, every one of them a specimen the creature could dominate.

Back on top, where it liked it. The creature slunk away, deeper into the darkness, picturing its own ambush that it would soon carry out in revenge. Stewing now with vague plans of murdering not one but two humans. And that filthy, inferior dog-thing.

19

Earlier, before nightfall, before the creature had left its safe haven in the concave tree trunk, Lee Bodkin and Gladdis Montrose stood near each other, motionless. Listening. Peering ahead into the swamp's greenery, eyes searching at ground level, then surveying back up into the heights of the massive cypress trees.

As they waited, Sheba returned from the dark morass of wetland. The dog looked at Bodkin, then back to the swamp from the direction she'd just come. Then up, and to the sides, holding her nose up to scent the air to the maximum. She glanced for a moment at Montrose, and again returned her gaze to Bodkin.

"Looks like you came up empty handed like us, girl," Bodkin said to the dog. It was apparent that Sheba could find no trace of the hostile beast. They'd hoped she would catch a scent of it, but if that furry monster thing stayed up high amongst the tree branches, smelling it out would be next to impossible. As would seeing it, if it crouched in a thick pocket and held still. The creature was darker than the trees, but not than the shadows. The shadows would thus envelope and conceal it from human eyes.

While Sheba had searched in the thickness, Bodkin and Montrose had stopped moving, trying to detect the slightest movement. It had been fruitless. No more dramatic monster escape leaps, no more cracking branches or snapping vines.

Sheba soon looked away from Bodkin, and Montrose took her turn to look over at him.

"Trail's gone cold, bud," Montrose said.

Bodkin nodded, still studying the organic mass ahead.

"I should have nailed that thing," Montrose said.

"Consider those your warmup shots," Bodkin said.

"Terrence Powell," she said.

Bodkin's attentiveness directed toward the shadows, the moss-covered tree branches, and the leafy forest floor started to vanish. His countenance changed accordingly as he looked at his partner. A new concern washed over it.

"He could still be alive," Montrose said.

Bodkin took one more half-glance at the swamp ahead, nodded again, and put the thick revolver away between his waistband and the small of his back.

"I recently was considering how simple life would be if one was a sociopath. No guilt or concern for anyone other than yourself," Bodkin said.

"Uh-huh. Being a psychopath would work too," Montrose said, clicking on the safety and maneuvering the rifle crosswise over her back.

"Yeah. Even lower anxiety than a sociopath, too," Bodkin said. "Would be extra nice."

"But we're stuck being normal."

"Speak for yourself," Bodkin said. They started their scramble-slither through the dense weeds, making scarcely a sound. Away from the creature, and toward the brutalized body of Terrence Powell.

***

Yep, they were still stuck being normal. Gladdis Montrose had been correct when she'd said that, and now she demonstrated it. She looked down once more at Terrence Powell, his body sprawled out, twisted, and very, very dead. She let an exasperated breath out as she looked away, toward the wilderness, wishing she weren't here.

"So the people observing this overall situation think it might be one of those furry forest wanderers?" Montrose asked. "Like a Bigfoot or Sasquatch or whatever?"

"That's the popular theory," Bodkin said.

"They're wrong. I'm no expert, but the Sasquatch is supposed to be a gentle critter, never attacking people," Montrose said. "And mellow in general. That freak we chased was like some kind of super beast. With fangs. It went from tree to tree like it was on an invisible trampoline or something."

"Yup. Between the three of us, we could barely keep track of the leapfrogging," Bodkin said. "And this brute here certainly does attack." He looked down at Powell's figure, natty outdoor duds still in place, seemingly ready to tackle anything. But wiped away from the land of the living in seconds. "The town's body count is already growing, and the area population is negligible in these parts. Not that many people to grab, you would think." He looked back at Montrose. "Not that many for a monster to kill. For now. Wait 'til the spring breakers get here."

Montrose looked upward, to the clouds, to nothing, the exasperation on her face growing, a little anguish creeping in. Spring break crowd meets killer wild thing. "God, why didn't I connect with just one shot," she said. "Like in the center of that big fat head on its shoulders."

"Not sure how much fat is there, tell ya the truth," Bodkin said. "When it smashed into me in our first clash it felt more like a boulder." Bodkin looked back down at Powell. "You'll get another chance," he said to Montrose. "We'll get the thing."

Montrose watched Bodkin as he crouched near Powell, examining something on the ground. Then scrutinizing further as he looked on Powell's body. He then picked a couple of specks off of the corpse, then a couple more off the ground. He held them toward Montrose, and she stepped forward, finally recognizing the miniscule items.

Specks of fur.

Bodkin took out the fillet knife from his front pocket. He removed the razor sharp blade from the leather sheath, and dropped the fur remnants into the compartment. Then he eased the knife back into the sheath, trapping the fur strands, and placed the tool back deep in the front of his hunting trousers.

"Evidence of some kind?" Montrose said.

"I'll show you when we get back to my room," Bodkin said.

They looked at Powell for a few more seconds, two experts at search-and-rescue standing over a pulverized body, helpless to do anything. No first aid has ever been effective for a crushed skull.

"Time to call in the cavalry?" Montrose said.

Bodkin nodded once, and slipped out his phone. A few moments later he spoke into it. "Sergeant Morton. Uh, been better. Say, I know you had the pleasure of meeting one Terrence Powell yesterday. Yeah, I guess that's one way you could describe him. The guy that had the huge ego."

Bodkin paused a few seconds, listening, then said to Morton, "No, I meant to say it that way. Had. Past tense."

20

Irwin Kagel formed the wrong impression immediately. In the late afternoon sun, he saw them stepping from a faded green pickup truck toward the front of the compound. He watched the macho man, Lee Bodkin, with wide shoulders prowling along as his protein supplement pectorals led the way. Yes, impressive, but secondary now. Bodkin's wolf hybrid pet behind him, alert like usual, calm but surveying for activity behind them every few moments. Nice, but still, secondary. It was the lovely vision of female power who strode along with him that locked in Kagel's attention.

Contained, petite power. Maybe half Bodkin's size overall. Tiny but pronounced muscles on her arms and shoulders, a fluff of hair flipping around in a ponytail behind her head. Her upper body was hugged by an old grey tank top designed in the classic beer memorabilia style: *Two Harbors Lager* it looked like from here. Never heard of it, but Kagel already liked the brew, seeing as the athletic woman was sporting its logo. She looked like some kind of fantastic, blonde, fit party girl.

Was this an introduction of sorts? To her? If so, this Bodkin guy was more awesome than he'd already pictured. But…ah, probably just one of his squeezes, flown in from up north, or from wherever. This lady pal of his looked Scandinavian more or less; from there perhaps? Kagel reached up and tried to straighten the silver tufts of hair sprouting out over each of his ears. No use. He dropped his hands.

Kagel reminded himself to not get his hopes up, like so many times before. After all, Bodkin had said he had a steady girlfriend up in Minnesota, like a fiancée almost. Bodkin had implied that fiancée bit at least, never came out and said it for sure. Evasive. Just like Kagel himself. Kagel appreciated that fact.

But if Bodkin wasn't making a social call in one way or another…why were they here? A vision of Tuma popped into Kagel's head, but he expunged it quickly.

Neither Bodkin nor the small woman he walked with looked straight at the front entrance. They'd glance ahead, then float their attention to either side of the compound, to the edges near the ground, and even complete a couple of glances at the roof. All casual and relaxed, as if they'd done it for years, their routine every time they made a visit someplace. Kagel's impression started to change as he watched. It aligned closer to the truth with each second.

Why had that thought come to him so naturally? Every time they made a visit? A visit to where? To a job where they'd vanquish other people? Who was she? Kagel watched her body move, feminine but under muscular control, the gymnast about to leap the pommel horse.

Then Kagel saw the handgun on her hip. A solid, plain nylon holster ensconcing a dense grayish black pistol handle. Evidently not just a party girl.

It was apparently…Bodkin's partner. The one the government reports claimed had more confirmed kills than Bodkin himself. What was the deal here? Why were they visiting? No call, no warning. Kagel's gut filled with butterflies. How much did they know?

Having no choice, Kagel scurried to the door, opening it before they could knock. He smiled as best he could.

"Good afternoon, Dr. Kagel," Bodkin said.

Kagel fell over himself with polite niceties, offering a nod to Bodkin, soothing comments to Sheba, and an elongated handshake and genuflection of the head to Gladdis Montrose.

"Got a few minutes to talk?" Bodkin said.

"Um, sure. A bit busy, but…"

"Let's set aside a few minutes, shall we?" Bodkin said, stepping into Kagel's facility before the doctor was even done gesturing for them to come inside.

Montrose also stepped inside and away from the two men, looking at the large, firmly locked doors at the end of the clinic. She noticed Sheba scenting the air in that direction, not alarmed but somewhat transfixed. Montrose then looked away from the dog, and in the direction of Kagel and Bodkin, looking at nothing in particular, hands resting calm but ready on her hips. Near the semi-automatic pistol holstered there.

"Can I, uh, get you folks anything," Kagel stammered. "I have a bottle of rum. Well, half a bottle."

He watched Bodkin step to a clinic table and move a couple of folders resting on its surface out of the way. From his pocket Bodkin removed a folded over Dixie cup. The top was covered with a transparent sandwich bag, secured there with a rubber band. Without a word, Bodkin popped off the sandwich bag and emptied the contents of the cup on the clinic table.

Little strands of dark fur. A type of fur Irwin Kagel recognized at once.

"Maybe these remnants look familiar to you. When you clean your lab, I'd bet you come across this type of hair now and then," Bodkin said.

Bodkin looked at Kagel, who in turn shrugged. Holding back, considering what to say.

Then Bodkin reached into his other pocket. He removed his fillet knife, covered with its sheath, and withdrew the shiny blade with a whisper of steel on leather. Kagel saw the sharp edge and gasped, in an instant mistaking the reason Bodkin was drawing a knife. He felt relief, a little anyway, when Bodkin set the blade on the table. The relief started to reverse itself when Bodkin tipped up the sheath, sprinkling the fur strands inside the makeshift container onto the table. Next to the ones already there…pieces of fur that looked exactly the same.

"Whatta ya think, good doctor?" Bodkin said. "Is that a match, or what? Slightly different, perhaps at the molecular level. I can't tell, not being an expert in hairy swampland killers. Your thoughts?"

Kagel started to raise his hands, dropped them, and said nothing.

"The hairs in the Dixie cup were tracked along on my boots, and dropped off in my motel room. The only place down here that I'd worn the boots was here to your lab. They'd been packed away up 'til that point."

"So, these here…" Kagel began, pointing at the second smattering of hairs.

"You want to know where they came from, I bet," Bodkin said. Kagel nodded.

"You remember hearing about a hotshot researcher coming to town, I'd assume," Bodkin said. "Terrence Powell."

"Yes, from the Enlighten Institute," Kagel said. Bodkin was on a roll, but was secretly surprised at the look of dismay, of horrified anticipation, on Kagel's face with the mention of Terrence Powell. Bodkin and Montrose had come to the compound with a presumption that Kagel was the culprit in some kind of murder scheme, or the villain who'd purposely unleashed something upon the innocent. That look of revulsion

Kagel just displayed, involuntarily, didn't go along with the plotting mad scientist stereotype. Bodkin continued.

"Well, Terrence Powell must now be referred to as 'the late Terrence Powell.' The hairs here," Bodkin said, pointing to the second sampling, "Were strewn all over the area where Powell was killed, out in the wetland. And on his body, stuck to his clothes no less. Gladdis, Sheba, and I trailed him in secret, as he went out to look for the beastly thing. Our swamp killer pal spoiled the event. We got there a few seconds too late, as it turned out."

"So he's dead," Kagel said, his shoulders visibly slumping.

"Very much so, sir," Bodkin said.

"Initially nobody let me know he was here...once I found out, I told them Powell was to meet with me. To be informed about what he was facing. Those cops, those damned idiots!" Kagel said, with emotion Bodkin hadn't expected. Kagel raised both hands up to his face, and buried it in them. Didn't look to Bodkin like a person who'd plotted someone else's demise.

Kagel soon removed the hands from his face, tightly crossed his arms over his chest. He stared at the floor for one long minute; he'd looked like he was about to cry, but didn't. Bodkin had a hunch for some reason that the guy was all cried out. The misery and regret were still there, somewhat, but Bodkin could see the slightly built researcher was building up a head of steam.

"Doctor," Bodkin began.

"Give me a fucking second, tough guy," Kagel said, clenching his jaws. Yep, a head of steam, now about to blow. Bodkin was actually relieved by it. He could relate. Plus, a scoundrel would be more likely to keep pretending everything was all right, mimicking cheer. They waited another 15 seconds, then Kagel began.

"So, it's time. Time to divulge the complete situation here," Kagel said.

Both Bodkin and Montrose maintained eye contact with Kagel, saying nothing.

Kagel looked a bit jittery, a little miserable. But simultaneously reclaiming control, anger still in place but diffusing rapidly. He continued. "I've been meaning to tell someone, for the longest time. Someone who could help."

"Pretend that we're here to help," Bodkin said. Kagel eyed Bodkin with disapproval for a moment, the annoyed school teacher with the brilliant but cheeky student.

"OK. Where to begin," Kagel said, taking a breath. "It all started in Africa."

"Started in Africa?" Montrose said, softly with a hint of doubt. She and Bodkin exchanged glances, neither expecting this twist.

Kagel looked at her and nodded, then gazed at the floor again. His eyebrows raised up, and he almost looked happy for a second. Then a tiny hint of returning despair wiped the cheer away. Something bittersweet was going on with those memories.

"Yes, Africa. Seems like only yesterday," Kagel said.

"Pray tell," Bodkin said.

21

"Our headquarters was based in Cameroon, but our camps were mobile and set up in a variety of spots," Kagel said. "Our task was to save Mountain Gorillas. They face countless risks from nature, always have. But over time, a different risk arose: a threat to their very existence. Poaching of these wonderful apes started to take off. The illegal hunting of them still goes on today. We couldn't complete the task of saving them, to summarize."

"Who's we?" Bodkin said.

"I was the chief researcher; a colleague of mine and I rounded out the science-based side. Just two of us. We had a great team of rescuers though, I think thirteen of them, ready to carry out any task we assigned. Not easy in the wilds of Africa."

"Were the poachers actually eating the gorillas?"

"Maybe in some cases. But that wasn't the main idea. Nothing nearly as necessary or honest as that. The poachers mainly wanted gorilla body parts to sell in the cities and towns," Kagel said. "It goes on in more than one place in Africa. Ever see a program or read up on the ape body parts industry over there?"

"I've heard a little about it," Bodkin said.

"The Gorillas in the Mist deal," Montrose said.

"Yes, exactly. Although in that movie they didn't detail the crisis nearly enough. Like the extent to which they wipe out entire gorilla families just to sell the body parts."

"Even the hands are chopped off for souvenirs, it's rumored," Montrose said.

"More than a rumor, sadly. Hands, feet, heads of murdered gorillas. All commonly for sale in their local markets. Mostly as novelties. Disgusting. Anyway, we were hired by a collaborative project. Greenpeace, the World Wildlife Fund, the United Nations. PETA too, although when it came time to pitch in financially, PETA never would cough up any dough. Oh well. The U.N. is still the anchor for funding of related projects."

"You still trying to save the Mountain Gorilla?" Bodkin said.

"Yes, although the efforts against poaching are reduced now. Due to the reality of the poachers in those areas."

"How so?" Bodkin said.

"The poachers switched from gorilla hunting and started killing off the rescue team. My long-time colleague and strategist on this whole anti-poaching effort, the one I just mentioned, was one of the victims."

"Terrible," Montrose said.

"To say the least. He managed to evade the killers with machetes and escape camp, but another poacher got him with an AK-47 back in the bush," Kagel said.

Just picturing it, the fatigue grew in Bodkin's face a little more. But regardless, he and Gladdis had to get the complete picture here. Either that, or simply get the hell out of town. He pushed on. "Were your efforts for saving the gorillas focused right there in Cameroon?"

"Somewhat, although gorillas are not as numerous there. Populations in both the Congo and in Uganda are greater. Those regions were our main focus."

"OK. So how does this tie in with the beastly thing that's terrorizing people here in Chicola?" Bodkin said.

"Let's get this out of the way right now: the beastly thing out there, as you say, is named Tuma. He's an ape named Tuma."

"So it's simply an ape?"

"Not simply, not by any means."

"Seemed like the thing we encountered had more to it than just a zoo animal would. Not just a chimp, not really a gorilla. Hard to know what we faced, even after seeing it up close with our own eyes…"

"Try listening first, with your own ears. OK?" Kagel said.

"Got it. All ears," Bodkin said.

"You're right. Tuma is not just a chimp, and not just a gorilla. He's a combination of both. Plus some other things," Kagel said.

Huh?

"Crazy jungle romance? What's the story?" Bodkin said.

Kagel looked at Bodkin for a two-count, that aura of disapproval in his glance enough to shut Bodkin up for the moment. The professor now had the floor.

"Tuma is the result of a chimpanzee father and a Mountain Gorilla mother. Each was carefully selected and nurtured, and then they were isolated together just before sexually maturing. So the breeding was not that surprising, being a two-ape family as they were."

They were all quiet for a moment, Bodkin and Montrose digesting what they'd just heard, Kagel looking forward to telling more.

"So the two different species were set up to breed purposely," Montrose said.

"They were, yes. And if you're wondering what the point was, well, it began as an attempt at a solution to save the hunted Mountain Gorillas. A security presence that could be nearby in the same hills, forests, and mountains as the persecuted gorillas. An ever-present guardian angel. The ultimate protector of the Mountain Gorilla."

"Gorillas are bigger, way bigger, than chimpanzees. Why mix up this guardian angel line with a smaller creature?" Bodkin said.

"You know most gorillas are primarily herbivores, I presume," Kagel said.

Montrose nodded affirmative. "Pretty much just grapes, berries, other fruit, and leaves, as I understand it," Bodkin said.

"Yes. Add to that a bunch of choice bugs, and you've got the ideal gorilla diet. But the chimpanzee is different. Much, much different," Kagel said. "Did you know that?"

Montrose shrugged, and Bodkin simply looked back at Kagel. He didn't know one way or another, but was sure Kagel would now fill them in.

"Much different," Kagel said again, pleased to lecture on the topic. "They'll eat anything and everything that a gorilla does, but oh so much more."

"Don't tell us meat," Bodkin said.

"Nothing satisfies them quite as much," Kagel said. "Did you know a team of wildlife biologists just a few years ago documented a pack of chimps on a leopard hunt?"

"Hadn't heard about it, no," Bodkin said, feigning disinterest. He actually wanted to hear this one, however.

"In this particular case, the chimps tracked down the cubs of a mother leopard. Chased the mother away, ate the cubs," Kagel said.

"Chased away a leopard," Bodkin said, looking incredulous.

"It's a fact. Well-documented study, commonly discussed in my circle. Events like that happen all the time in the chimpanzee world. Chimps, especially mature males, can be more violent than most people would ever believe. They sometimes kill other chimpanzee families, for that matter."

"So not quite like Cheetah from the Tarzan movies," Montrose said.

"Heavens no," Kagel said. "They used a toddler chimpanzee for those films, by the way. That's nothing at all what a mature chimp looks like. Especially not an old male."

"Is this Tuma freak–" Bodkin began.

"Ape," Kagel said.

"Ape…is he now an old male?" Bodkin said.

"No. Wish he were. Rather, he's in his prime. He's the analogous of the 19-year-old testosterone-ridden rowdy punk tearing around town in the faded old pickup truck."

"Hey, I tear all over the country in a faded old pickup truck," Bodkin said.

"OK, then tearing around in a sports car. Or a Dukes of Hazzard muscle car. Whichever you prefer," Kagel said.

"Got it. So that's why his strength is so…profound I guess you could say," Bodkin said. "That, plus the chimp ferocity and gorilla muscle fibers pitching in."

"Uh, yes, those factors. Plus one other major one."

Bodkin and Montrose exchanged glances again. Possibly gonna get weirder.

"To describe it in brief," Kagel said, "I rather doubt, at the peak of his treatment, that he would have passed the drug testing so prevalent in sports today."

Yep, weirder.

"Catch my drift?" Kagel said.

"I do. I believe we both do. So, what kind of anabolic steroid did you boost your beast with?" Bodkin said.

"Dianabol," Kagel said.

"Ah. No second rate substances for the Tuma project, in other words."

"No. Straight to the high octane gas. The strength gains were almost indescribable. So my colleague and I, against our better judgment, decided to keep going with the Dianabol injections."

"Indescribable. Apt description," Montrose said, thinking of the ape creature bounding from tree to tree with little effort.

"And I concur that it was against your better judgment," Bodkin said. "Gladdis and I can both attest to the steroids jumpstarting the beast's leaping ability. I nearly caught up to the thing after it scrambled into a big cypress. Jumped clear over to another tree before I could give it a helping of hollow points."

"You climbed up after Tuma?" Kagel said

"Don't underestimate his gymnastic abilities," Montrose said. "Bodkin's lazy, cool posture thing is mostly an act, Dr. Kagel. Started it long ago, as part of his method for approaching girls."

"Did it work?" Kagel asked. "You don't seem jealous," he said to Montrose. "Oh, wait. Are you two even–," Kagel stammered.

"Victims. Tuma. Steroids. Killer ape. People running and screaming," Bodkin said to Kagel.

Kagel wiped his face clean of the awkward moment, becoming the professor again. "Yes. So, as I was saying. He was to protect the endangered gorillas and destroy those that hunted them. We knew he would face the grave danger of guns, so we trained him accordingly. To fear guns, but not to retreat for good. To evade, hide, and wait. Then to attack with ruthless force."

"I've experienced a live demonstration," Bodkin said.

"And not to just attack, not in a straightaway, face-to-face fight. But rather to use stealth," Kagel said, his eyes lit up now.

"Now you're speaking our language," Bodkin said. "What stealth methods did your team teach?"

"Oh, several. But none greater than the one that encourages humans to miss with their guns, to flee, to lose their spirit. And that's something an ape, especially one endowed such as Tuma, can do better than almost any other mammal," Kagel said.

"And that is?"

"To attack from above. Silently."

The vision of that enhanced ape beast out there in the dense Florida swamp, dropping with all its weight and bloodthirsty fangs, without a sound, was indeed unsettling.

"What if the people on the ground simply picked off the ape as it jumped down?" Montrose said. "Blasted it?"

"What if there were more than one Tuma?" Kagel said. "More. That was our grand plan. Chimps are well known for pack hunting, for coordinating their group movements in perfect concert on escaping prey. Once the prototype, which we'd hoped Tuma would be, was perfected, we planned to breed them and breed them. Then a couple of them getting shot, while sad, wouldn't stop the effort dead. And the fear factor to the poachers, after just an attack or two, would have been significant."

"If there were any poachers left," Bodkin said.

"Well said." Kagel smiled at that thought. "We wanted to get our perfect specimen to protect and cherish fellow apes. To live near them, and with them. And aside from their masters, to despise human beings with intensity. We used advanced psychological encouragement to that end even while Tuma was but a baby."

"Nurture trumps nature. To despise humans…with enough vitriol to kill them?" Bodkin said.

"More or less," Kagel said. "As you see, in our most hopeful specimen, Tuma, we got half of that wish list right."

"Yeah, the kill-the-human part does seem intact. So, you bred and conditioned a perfectly athletic specimen, then threw in that chemical twist, and we're stuck with the killing machine we have today," Bodkin said. "One with a fetish for sinking its fangs into skulls."

"Oh, you mean Tuma killing people with a skull bite…because of the steroids?" Kagel said.

"Just a thought," Bodkin said.

"No, no. The steroids detour from nature was just another planned enhancement. Made him more powerful of course, but really, it was a minor tweak," Kagel said.

"Minor tweak. You've got the euphemisms down, Doctor," Bodkin said.

"Trust me, the steroid treatments were minor. Compared to what we'd done to Tuma before that," Kagel said. "Compared to the other substance we'd injected him with."

His audience waited. Getting weirder. And weirder.

"We did other, more strategic injections while Tuma was still a newborn," Kagel said. "The treatments were risky, but we felt it necessary. Considering what had happened to our other specially bred specimens, dying from a variety of diseases, we felt some preventive action needed to take place."

"What were you trying to prevent?" Montrose said.

"Infections, mainly. Malaria was another risk. Which, by the way, is my main research focus now at this compound," Kagel said. "For beating strains that kill people, and related types that afflict apes. New strains appear all the time.

And with Tuma's special purpose, we needed the most effective agent known to humankind to battle infections. Those from bugs, snakes, superficial bullet wounds. Heck, other apes. Especially those chimps, in case one bit Tuma."

Kagel paused, thinking.

"So, the stuff you injected. Was it some kind of special serum you cooked up?" Montrose said.

"No, the injected matter was completely natural. But, as it turned out, had effects that were completely horrific," Kagel said. He looked at the ceiling, appearing detached for a moment. As if dreaming…or maybe reviewing a nightmare. Then he continued.

"To make his system as hardy as could be, to fight off myriad infections, as an infant Tuma was given infusions from the blood of the Botswana Gliding Bat."

"That's some kind of robust bat?" Bodkin asked.

"To say the least. The Botswana Gliding Bat has the inborn genetic makeup to fight off disease better than any mammal that we know of. So its blood seemed like the top choice to blend into our new ape's system. And yes, Tuma's resistance was tested and proved to be phenomenal. But…"

"Another but. Here we go," Bodkin said.

"Something unforeseen developed. The DNA of the bat, somehow, resulted in Tuma acquiring unexpected urges."

Kagel looked at the ceiling once again, clenched his fists, released them, then looked back at Bodkin and Montrose.

"The fact is, the Botswana Gliding Bat has the special ability to sink its long fangs into the heads of other creatures. Small prey at times, and more commonly into the heads of carrion. Like dead wildebeest, gazelles, cattle and such."

"So, it likes brains," Bodkin said.

"Yes, mainly the crucial fluids found there. The bat partly depends on those nutrients to survive. To live out a healthy life."

"The brains of carrion. As opposed to the smaller critters it pierces, which I assume are still alive when it does it to them," Bodkin said.

"They often are, yes."

Kagel held out his hands, palms up, seeking understanding.

"You see, the Botswana Gliding Bat is a type of vampire bat."

22

"You'll need an additional partner," Kagel said.

"I don't think so," Bodkin said.

"Yes, you do need one. And a very special partner is willing to assist you. Guide you, actually."

"We don't need a guide," Bodkin said.

"You lost his trail already. You probably will again, and it could cost you your life if he backtracks. You're limited to mobility on the ground, Tuma can navigate the heights like a gull floating above the beach."

"I can climb. Gladdis is even better. You might be surprised," Bodkin said.

"As fast of a climber as the animal you pursued?"

"Of course not; we're human."

"So you rely on guns. Understandably. But while climbing, and holding on while up in a tree, can you reliably shoot?"

"Um, definitely no," Bodkin said.

"So your team could use a better climber," Kagel said.

Bodkin and Montrose said nothing, their attention now focused on where the doctor was going with this.

"As well as a better scent tracker. Or, one more specific to what you're now hunting," Kagel said. "The scent of Tuma, in the upper reaches of cypress trees."

"This girl has the nose of a blood hound," Bodkin said, nodding at Sheba.

"But up in the trees? At the level of the upper branches? There are scent streams down low, but also separate ones way at the top," Kagel said.

"We're both deer hunters. We grasp the concept," Montrose said.

The steam was building in Kagel's head again, and showing in his eyes.

"So, yes or no. Are you serious about taking on this assignment, and seeing it through to the end?"

"You sound like my high school football coach," Bodkin said.

"Yes or no?" Kagel said.

"We're still here, aren't we?"

"Then wait where you are, while I prepare your new partner for the introduction," Kagel said. Before they could reply, or for that matter leave the premises and never come back, Irwin Kagel went to the high-security doors at the back of the clinic. He removed a remote control from his pocket, and pressed a button on it once. A sharp unlocking sound traveled through the clinic before Kagel swung open one of the doors. Without looking back, he stepped through and pulled the door shut behind him.

As a second clack popped gently upon the door locking, Bodkin and Montrose looked for a moment at each other, relaxed where they stood, and smoothly drew their handguns. With weapons dangling at ease, they waited.

23

"Mr. Bodkin, Ms. Montrose…prepare to be alarmed," said Irwin Kagel.

The two of them watched Kagel, feeling both curiosity and caution. Each glanced for a second at the high-security door leading to the back of the facility; Kagel had left it ajar an inch or so.

"And please put away your weapons," Kagel continued. "There will be no need for them."

"Um. That depends," Bodkin said.

"I assure both of you, you are in absolutely no danger here," Kagel said. "Not from me, nor my partner. Whom you are now about to meet."

"I guess we'll find out one way or another." Both Bodkin and Montrose had already checked on Sheba's posture and overall behavior. Alarm was not apparent in either, even with the large door cracked open. Sheba could smell whatever circulated from back there just like a person walking into a bakery could smell fresh bread. But no anxiety was registering with the dog. Bodkin felt reassured by the fact, but only slightly.

Bodkin established eye contact with Gladdis then, in a silent communication routine they were used to. He had to make sure she wanted to go ahead with stepping through the door and entering Kagel's secret area in back. If not, they'd leave now. Bodkin recognized an affirmative signal, ever so subtle, from her eyes and facial expression. He looked back to Kagel.

"Please put your guns away, and we'll proceed with the meeting," Kagel said.

"Are we meeting another person?"

"No."

"Your partner's not human?"

"No."

"Then dream on. We'll step in there, after you of course. But the guns stay out," Bodkin said.

Kagel thought about the situation for a few seconds, looking ill at ease…worried, actually. He appeared to be hiding nothing. The chance of something diabolical being in the works did in fact seem remote, but the whole scenario was approaching the bizarre. The guns would stay out.

"Suit yourself," Kagel said finally. "But if either of you lose your cool for some reason and raise your weapon to shoot, I'll jump in the way to protect my partner. He's the only family I have left, you could say."

"First, assure us the door will be left open," Bodkin said.

Kagel pointed his remote control at the door. After pressing a button, a deadbolt inside the door shot out with a thwack, preventing the door from shutting fully. The deadbolt was copper in color and looked thick enough to support the weight of a lift bridge. Nothing was light duty in Kagel's compound.

"One more question before we follow you in there, Doctor," Bodkin said.

"Go ahead," Kagel said.

"Whatever we're about to meet or interact with back there…does it have anything to do with your project over in Africa?"

"Oh yes," Kagel said. "*Everything* to do with the project in Africa."

24

Kagel again went through the door at the back of the clinic, this time holding it for Bodkin. Bodkin clutched it with his free hand, and with the other signaled Sheba in ahead of him with the barrel of his revolver. The dog whisked through the doorway without a sound, on high alert.

Montrose grabbed the door next. Instead of stepping through, she pushed her back up against the door, leaning into it and propping it wide open. She kept one foot back inside the clinic, and the other on the floor of the unknown portion of the facility. Watching both directions. At least at first.

Bodkin took in the entirety of the enormous room, more or less a gymnasium, for the first several seconds. He took one look to his right, and without hesitation circled behind Kagel, into a position now to the other side of the doctor. Bodkin stayed completely behind him, as to watch both Kagel and the being resting on the floor just beyond the researcher.

What Bodkin had first laid eyes upon when entering the spacious facility was impressive. Telling too, suggesting much of what went on back here.

Sections of tree branches, most the thickness of hefty logs, networked from the floor to a level up near the ceiling. They looked real, but they may have been artificial replicas, hard to tell. It wouldn't really matter, if they were used for what Bodkin assumed. The logs and dense branches had been fused together somehow, probably with an industrial glue of some type, to form a realistic simulation of an indoor forest.

The section straight ahead upon entering, maybe 60 feet from where he stood, held an authentic re-creation of a rocky slope. The faux stony hill started at the floor and rose up at a 45-degree angle to within just a few feet of the 20-foot high ceiling. The surfaces had been smoothed and engineered to appear genuine in color and texture.

From a couple of the massive branches hanging over the man-made slope, two farm tractor tires dangled from heavy ropes. The ropes looked like they'd been stressed and twisted over and over again, but still intact.

The area directly in front of where they'd entered took up about a fourth of the whole gymnasium-like facility. To the left stood a bare wall, maybe 50 feet from the door, with only a sink and small refrigerator located along it. Forgettable.

What lay to the right, however, commanded immediate attention. Just 30 feet from where they'd come through the door, a long, solid wall of steel bars formed the boundary. It was a cage, running the length of the wall on that side. The bars extended fully to the ceiling.

A rolling door, around six feet wide, had been installed in the center of the cage. The door had been rolled all the way to the left, and was thus wide open.

On the floor, at the door of the cage, waited a massive gorilla, poised on all fours. Looking nearly as wide as the cage's opening, and staring out at them.

25

"This is my friend and partner, Ragnor. He's going to help you find and vanquish our current killer at large," Kagel said.

"That so?" Bodkin said.

"If you know what's good for you, yes. For your own protection, and to take the advantage away from your prey," Kagel said. He looked at Bodkin, waiting for a response. But Bodkin said nothing, still peering at the motionless gorilla. The ape looked straight at Bodkin, then at Montrose in the doorway, and then at Sheba. The dog currently seemed to hold most of the gorilla's attention.

"Whatever you do, don't confuse Ragnor here with the hostile beast that is Tuma," Kagel said.

"I won't. This one is bigger," Bodkin said.

"He is. He certainly is. He's a Mountain Gorilla, and a silverback at that. It's the largest any gorilla on earth can get," Kagel said. "So yeah, he's huge. But under normal circumstances, gorillas aren't dangerous to humans. Giving and receiving kindness is more the norm."

"So I've seen on TV," Bodkin said "Those kindness traits still in place with our ape giant here?"

"Yes. I assure you. See much aggression in him?" Kagel said, looking at the gorilla. The ape looked back, intent but with a neutral expression. "He's in control, and obedient. Currently he's awaiting my permission to step from the cage."

"If he has so little animosity in him, what good is he to Gladdis and me?"

"He stores aggressiveness deep inside, trust me. And he has no affection for his distant cousin, Tuma," Kagel said. "In fact, you can rest assured Ragnor here wants him dead. And Ragnor wants to be involved with the killing, hands-on. Ready for contact?"

"As in kinder, gentler contact?"

"If you want to become friends with Ragnor, he'll accept," Kagel said.

"Why would he?"

"Ragnor has been informed about your intentions. That you are his assistants in his quest, the ones who will help him catch Tuma. To catch Tuma, and to kill him."

"Your gorilla understands what you're saying?"

"My friend understands enough," Kagel said.

"Hard to believe."

"From the time he was weaned off his mother, he's had more contact with humans than he's had with apes."

"Sounds like a fast learner."

"I don't know exactly how old you are, Mr. Bodkin, but I'd bet Ragnor is not much younger."

"I didn't know they could live that long," Bodkin said.

"There's a lot you don't know, so please hear me out," Kagel said.

"Oh, and not sure I liked that part about us being the gorilla's assistants."

"I'm afraid that's the way he'll see it. He's a silverback, after all."

Bodkin took a breath, let it out, and looked over at Montrose. Her posture was still relaxed, her pistol still dangling in hand. Like a viper while it's in neutral, just before uncoiling to strike. She took in her own breath and raised her eyebrows. Bodkin recognized it as uncertainty. His call, per their established procedure.

He pictured the menacing hybrid ape attacking Sheba and him, after it had snuck up to watch over the grade school. Most likely there to kill kids. While thinking of this, he glanced over at the even larger gorilla. A tremble shuddered through Bodkin, and a hint of shortness of breath touched his chest. Then it was gone. He was again Lee Bodkin, the unstoppable. As long as he kept telling himself that.

OK.

"Let's get acquainted," Bodkin said.

Kagel turned toward the gorilla. "All right, big fella. Come over here and meet Mr. Bodkin."

The gorilla moved out of the cage. Its movement was a combination of churning, rolling, and rippling, as endlessly large, sculpted muscles flexed and relaxed. It navigated on all fours, leading its progression with a head as big as the Liberty Bell. Despite its obvious power, it looked at peace, and almost disinterested.

Sheba moved over next to Bodkin, watching the ape as it advanced. She was still not distressed, not in appearance anyway. Bodkin used her as the barometer in this situation. She glanced up at Bodkin, then back to the gorilla.

"It's OK, girl," Bodkin said to the dog as he reached down and stroked her side, not sure if his words were completely true.

The gorilla stopped in front of them. Bodkin thought he could smell the ape, its fur, probably its skin too. He didn't know for sure, as he'd never seen a gorilla in real life, except at the zoo back up in St. Paul. From 30 feet away, and through glass. Nothing like this. The scent was one of primordial power, of wildness…and of cleanliness. The well-bathed gorilla. Gotta hand it to Kagel.

The gorilla raised its right arm, and held its hand out to Bodkin.

"Hi there, big boy," Bodkin said to the ape. He felt a half-smile crease his face, before dropping off it. "What do I do here, Kagel? Shake its hand?"

"Just touch palms with him."

Bodkin wondered what life would be like with just one arm. He also reassured himself: he was the one holding a .357 magnum. Then he reached out with his left hand, and placed it in the gorilla's palm.

A soft texture like smooth leather met Bodkin's hand. The ape didn't clench its hand into a fist, didn't clamp down on Bodkin's hand and crush it. Although Bodkin didn't doubt that the primate could do just that if it chose to. Instead it closed its hand just enough to feel Bodkin's fully.

The gorilla looked up from their joined hands into Bodkin's eyes. It maintained eye contact with him for three seconds. Then it released Bodkin's hand and moved away, turning to face Sheba. It raised the same arm up to the dog, holding its open hand near her nose.

"It'll be fine, Sheba. He's with us," Bodkin said in the tone he often used to soothe her. Hoping like anything it was true.

Sheba hesitated for a couple of seconds, then moved forward, bumping her nose once into Ragnor's burly set of knuckles. Then the ape reached slowly forward, as if to pet the dog.

Again, Bodkin hoped for peace between the two beasts in front of him, in the half-second before the contact. The gorilla's wide hand stroked the fur of Sheba's neck, once, then twice. Ragnor went for a third repetition, but Sheba performed a gentle duck and whisked back next to Bodkin's leg. Enough was enough.

The gorilla looked at Sheba for a moment, then up to Bodkin. By the expression in its large, dark eyes, he could swear the ape had just had its feelings hurt.

"She's aloof. Get used to it," Bodkin said to Ragnor.

The gorilla looked at him for another one-count, sniffed, then veered a few feet toward the door to the clinic. Where Gladdis Montrose stood. She'd been previously watching both directions, out into the clinic, and back toward the gymnasium. She now only watched one: the direction leading straight to the ape.

"Move no further, Ragnor," Kagel said. The ape stopped at once. "Approach Ragnor if you'd like to greet him," Kagel said then to Montrose.

"He's not fond of those scenes in King Kong, is he?" Montrose said.

"With the maiden protected in the palm of his hand? The pretty blonde?" Kagel said, but Montrose was paying no attention, already closing the door gently to its extended deadbolt. Letting it close but making sure it stayed ajar.

She stepped forward toward Ragnor, and the ape approached to within a few feet. Ragnor did so with just a few motions of his muscle flexion-and-rolling style of ambulation, supporting most of his body weight with bridge pylon arms. The furry bulk with churning limbs moved with no sound across the concrete floor.

A bristly ape arm reached out once again, a slender human arm returned the gesture, and two palms touched. A few seconds later, the gorilla withdrew its hand and resumed its stance on all fours. It then simply gazed at Gladdis Montrose.

And kept gazing.

"I feel slighted," Bodkin said, nearly 30 seconds after the gorilla began its stare. "Ragnor never looked at me like that."

"Ms. Gladdis here is female, for one thing. Yes, to your question before, Gladdis," Kagel said. "There might be a little of that King Kong-type of fascination going on."

"Maybe you should get him a lady friend," Montrose said.

"He had one. They lived together in this very compound. She's unfortunately no longer with us. C'mon, you big oaf," Kagel said, the last sentence to Ragnor, waving the gorilla toward him.

"The female was transferred elsewhere? Or…" Montrose said.

"Dead."

"Natural causes?" Bodkin said, sensing the answer to that was negative.

"No. Killed. Hey, get over here, Ragnor."

"Let me venture a hypothesis," Bodkin said. "Big Ragnor here had a female partner once. At the present location. She has since been killed. Now burly Ragnor wants to destroy the other former resident of this place, a homicidal ape experiment named Tuma."

"On the right track, sir," Kagel said. Ragnor had just maneuvered near the doctor, and Kagel placed a caring hand on the ape's shoulder.

"Tuma killed Ragnor's bride," Bodkin said.

"You're truly a sleuth," Kagel said.

26

"Talk about an incentive for revenge."

"Nothing could whet the appetite for retribution more acutely," Kagel said. He gave one more caress upon the gorilla's shoulder before the massive beast floated away, using his soundless, muscular motion, eyes now on the tree branch matrix at the rear of the gymnasium.

"What happened exactly?" Bodkin said.

"Long story short," Kagel said.

"That's how we prefer it."

"So you're a man of few words."

"Mostly, except when detailing my fishing conquests. So what happened with Ragnor's partner?" Bodkin said.

"Well, we imported Tuma to this facility after I'd been over here for about a year. I was there in Africa to oversee Tuma's birth and all, and his initial training. I had to leave or be killed, as was the case with most everybody on the project," Kagel said. "Tuma had been kept in a Nigerian zoo enclosure during that separation." Kagel looked down and shook his head. "All alone."

"So he arrived here…" Bodkin said.

"Yes, and Ragnor and his mate were to be his family. That started off just fine. While Tuma was young enough. While still a kid, in human terms."

"It started off well and obviously didn't end that way."

"No," Kagel said. "They were both the disciplinarians of Tuma. And it was intended that Ragnor would help Tuma train and develop. It was simply family dynamics in the world of the gorilla. But because of

those other influences within Tuma, maybe the
crossbreeding itself…"

"Feisty Tuma didn't like being told what to do,"
Bodkin said.

"That's right," Kagel said, looking down again. This
time his face was strained, then it formed into a snarl. He
stomped his foot. "That unappreciative cocksucker! That
reject!"

Bodkin looked away from the doctor's rage, and
instinctively at Ragnor. Seeing if the big ape was coming
back from the tree branch jungle to protect its master.
Nope. The gorilla swung and navigated branch to
branch, a massive, muscled truckload of dark and silvery
hair moving around up there like an alley cat. He ignored
the raised voice of Kagel; apparently he wasn't quite like
the typical protective guard dog. In this case, thank
heavens.

"How did this culprit Tuma attack your ape's partner
and get away with it? Without Ragnor smashing him, I
mean," Bodkin said.

"Her name was Dara, by the way. 'Dara' means
'rejoice' in Nigerian. Fitting. A wonderful ape," Kagel
said. "God, what transpired was simply devious. The
cunning of that experimental mishap that I helped make.
Tuma, the schemer."

"What was the scheme?" Bodkin said, starting to lose
patience.

"The apes, all three of them, had returned from the
open space in back of the compound. Out getting sun
and fresh air. Back inside, ready to return to the caged
area. Which I usually leave open, just like the door to the
back yard when the weather's nice."

Bodkin looked to the top of the artificial rock
structure, and as described saw a wide door near the top,
currently closed. Same width as the cage door down on

the floor near them. Nothing too surprising to Bodkin; he'd expect some way to let the beasts in here navigate to the yard in back, to play outside. Pretty standard with pets, in his experience. Of course, these weren't standard pets.

"The cage door there," Kagel said, gesturing to the one Ragnor had recently crawled from. "It can be locked and unlocked by remote control, as you've seen."

"Yep."

"But the door can also be locked with a slam. Closed slowly, the lock won't latch into place. But if it gets shut with great momentum, by design it locks."

"So Tuma observed. And remembered," Bodkin said.

"Sadly, yes."

"I'm guessing Ragnor went into the cage first," Bodkin said.

"That's how it happened. Ragnor typically led the way, and Tuma knew it. The vindictive Tuma waited until the big guy was inside, then just smacked the cage door shut. Then swarmed on Dara," Kagel said. "He'd have attacked both of them, but I figure he didn't have the confidence to take on Ragnor. Not then, anyway."

"You were there?"

Kagel didn't answer at first, instead looking at the far end of the gymnasium, starting to zone out. Recalling horrors, most likely. Bodkin couldn't wait until this was all over. Go back up north, into the increasingly cold temps, head out on another assignment. Most likely hunting scumbags who were hiding out in the cold wilderness and swamps. Bad guys like terrorists, cannibals, psychos. Escaped convicts. More normal stuff.

"Yes, I was in fact here when it occurred," Kagel said. "Just over at the sink there, washing off a bucket of vegetables for the group. Tuma's attack was so sudden and unexpected. Besides every other dangerous aspect of his being, Tuma's a good actor. He'd been behaving as if everything was fine, most likely stewing with hatred inside."

"'Roid rage," Bodkin said.

"What?"

"A term in pop culture…some massive jocks, bodybuilders and football players mostly, are known to get edgy when abusing performance-enhancing drugs. To get quite irritable."

"Oh, the steroids you mean?"

"That would be them," Bodkin said.

"We just wanted to make him more capable," Kagel said, partly in apology. "Anyway, after the assault began, I ran out to the clinic, got my Taser stick. It's like a cop's Taser, except it extends eight feet on a pole. By the time I got back, Dara was dead and Tuma had leapt out of the open door to the back property."

"And not seen since, I gather," Bodkin said.

"No, not by me at least. Up and over the electrified security fence, gone. Absorbed a little electric shock to do it, I imagine. A high fence, but it's mostly to keep people and things out."

Kagel was fading, his body looking deflated.

"Let's drop that subject for now, shall we," the doctor said.

"As for the hunt tomorrow," Montrose said. "Suggestions on how to proceed?"

"I was going to get to that, glad you asked," Kagel said. "For starters, right nearby I've set out a burlap sack of edibles on a regular basis. Oranges, berries, coco plums, carrots, potatoes."

"Baiting it," Bodkin said.

"Yes, basically. And the bastard has hit the bait, over and over. I think he's been viewing the compound in secrecy…probably with longing. Tuma may still consider this place his home."

"So, right behind the compound," Bodkin said. "That's where the eager Tuma's been hanging out?"

"At times, for sure. Ragnor's went right up to where Tuma has posted. Spots in the trees with a clear view of the facility here. This big guy here's been disappointed that Tuma's already gone when we get there."

"So the two of you actually embarked on hunts for the killer beast?"

"Hunts? Not sure what to call it. The two of us went out, more than once. Right on Tuma's well-worn trail."

"Unarmed?"

"I've got the Taser stick I've mentioned. And Ragnor."

"Ragnor wasn't there to initiate a rekindling of friendship, I'd wager," Bodkin said.

"No."

"And neither are you, correct?"

"Tuma would kill me in five seconds," Kagel said.

"Not the dream stepfather to him, then?"

"Of course not. And Ragnor isn't either. Nor is he Tuma's brother or friend in any way. When we ventured into the swamp, Ragnor didn't want to give up the hunt. He's as hungry for Tuma's demise as Tuma is for mine."

"Ragnor versus that Tuma freak. Man, I can just picture the fur flying. If this was a movie I'd attend for sure," Bodkin said, smiling. Then he caught himself and made the smile recede. He could sense Gladdis looking over at him with disapproval. "Uh, a dangerous endeavor, what you did." Back to the subject, another quick Bodkin recovery.

"It was. I agonized over continuing the searches. But decided against it in the end. Because, I'm pretty certain, against Tuma, Ragnor would lose the fight."

"But this living mountain of muscle you've got here is even bigger than your killer product out there in the wetland," Bodkin said.

"*Product*. I like that. Although it hurts to be reminded that I'm mostly responsible for Tuma's existence. But, yes, Ragnor is bigger. Just as tall and much wider. But trust me, no stronger. Tuma's a powerhouse," Kagel said.

"Um, yeah, I got a sample of it personally. The punk punched me in the face."

"Sorry about that, really. But you just hinted at why Tuma is superior to even Ragnor in close-quarters combat. He knows how to fight."

"Plus those teeth," Montrose said.

"Oh, yes. The oversized fangs, part of that artificially infused heritage. The bat DNA and all. It could help decide the winner."

"Who taught this Tuma thing how to punch?" Bodkin said.

"Our group over in Cameroon. Basic stuff, using operant conditioning: correct punches rewarded, poor ones discouraged," Kagel said. "We had a bare knuckle boxer in our crew. A tough, wiry youngster, a Cameroon native."

"I hold that guy personally responsible for my bruised face," Bodkin said. "Contact him and let him know I challenge him to a bout."

"You sound pretty confident, Mr. Bodkin."

"That's because Lee's been known to cheat in fistfights," Montrose said. "His usual boxing form is to tackle, slam, and strangle unconscious."

"That could perhaps do the trick," Kagel said with a smirk, not able to fully relate. The biggest fight he'd ever engaged in personally was the removal of a cork from a wine bottle.

"So. Ragnor will lead you along the paths in the area. The primary baiting location is a mere 90 meters behind the compound, maybe 100 at the most. But from there it gets more complicated. A few trails meander back into the wetland, and snake out in a few directions. The big guy here will help you sniff out the signs."

"Wonderful. But you actually meant to say the gorilla will lead us?" Bodkin said.

"Naturally."

"I may not see it that way. Gladdis and I are the experienced hunters in this group. Seems a little backwards."

"Uh, it's for the best, believe me."

"He's special to you, Doctor, but to us he's just an ape," Bodkin said.

"Some of those trails are up in the trees. Not all are literally pounded-down paths in the muddy ground. So, see why you need Ragnor?"

This was getting tiring. Trails up in the trees.

"Seeing it more and more," Bodkin said. "Our prey's gonna wear us out."

"And maybe sneak attack you. He's part chimpanzee, remember. Those climbs and jumps don't mean much to Tuma."

"I suppose not. Big, mean, warped chimp. Plus so much more," Bodkin said.

"True. He's partly fueled by hate, so there's more urgency for his hostile actions than a chimp normally has. The infusions and injections played a part in getting him to this stage. He is a special specimen, no question. Speaking of which," Kagel said. "There's talk going around town, pretty silly really. The theory is that there's a real live Sasquatch in town. Not sure if you'd heard that or not."

"It's been mentioned," Bodkin said.

"But of course, what else could they conclude? If they knew the whole story behind Tuma, they'd be begging to have him replaced with Bigfoot."

"I'd take the trade," Bodkin said. "Do you think the Sasquatch of legend is real? Not here, but in some other place in the world."

"I lean toward yes. But hard to say for sure. Wish I had the time and money to do my own exploration for such a being. It would be fantastic. But that's not going to happen, not with the gorilla crisis so far from solved," Kagel said. "Priorities."

"Nobody can do it all," Bodkin said. "I can barely pull off a successful Florida vacation."

"Heh. I understand. Anyway, if there's a genuine Sasquatch in existence, someone will eventually come across it," Kagel said. "While on the subject: did you know Washington State has a Sasquatch-related rule in their books? It states that the harassing of Bigfoot, Sasquatch, or other undiscovered subspecies is a felony punishable by a fine or imprisonment."

"You don't say," Bodkin said.

"Someone must know something," Kagel said. "Oh yes, another thing. The awkward police officer, Sergeant Morton…you met him?"

"Uh-huh."

"Saw him at the café this morning," Kagel said. "He told me that tomorrow he's going out on a full-scale expedition for the killer. Out in the swamp. Alone, but with reinforced armaments."

"Meaning?"

"He said he's bringing a water bottle, a snack, and six extra bullets."

"When's Sergeant Morton commencing his journey?"

"He comes on his shift at noon. Said he hopes to have it all wrapped up in a couple of hours." Kagel looked at the two of them, and for the first time in this meeting, they all saw eye-to-eye. If Morton was allowed to proceed without help, he wasn't long for this world.

"We'll be going out first thing in the morning, regardless. Hopefully the danger to Morton will be averted by then," Bodkin said.

"Early sounds good. Ragnor is at his most energetic then. So, we might as well call it a day now," Kagel said. "Tomorrow morning's show time. Oh, and welcome to the Ape Gym, by the way."

"That's what you call this place?" Bodkin said.

"Yes. The Ape Gym," Kagel said.

"How original," Bodkin said.

"Hey, I'm a scientist, not an ad executive," Kagel said.

"How do you see this turning out?" Montrose said, looking at Kagel.

"You mean a pair of armed bounty hunters and their tracking dog, following the lead of their guide, a silverback gorilla? As they hunt for a simian killing machine?"

"Yep," Montrose said.

"How would I know? I've never heard of it being done before," Kagel said.

Montrose stared at him for a moment, then let her eyes roam the facility again.

"That offer of rum still good?" Bodkin said.

"Certainly is, certainly is. Let's leave the big guy here, and I'll fetch a couple of shot glasses out in the clinic area."

"Make it three, Kagel," Montrose said.

Irwin Kagel looked at her, and attempted a smile. He didn't hope for much. To his surprise, the ice of her countenance had melted, and she gently smiled back. Not a seductive one; more like, *we're on the same team now.*

With that, Kagel's spirit lifted. He led them out of the Ape Gym, back to the clinic, scurrying toward the rum.

27

On its quest for vengeance, the big silverback looked to be making a pretty smooth transition from supposedly peaceful to definitely dangerous. Lee Bodkin watched Ragnor rolling and crawling, climbing and prowling, navigating fallen trees and groundcover greenery. Obvious that his heavy, powerful body was clearly made for this very task.

The ape would periodically stop and examine the forest with a burning focus, treetop to treetop, then down the trunks to lower branches. The neutral look on its face that they'd encountered upon first meeting the gorilla was now gone. A percolating intensity had replaced it.

The gorilla looked to be in fierce warrior mode. Even as he crawled, plowed, and stepped along, Ragnor had entered a zone of deep concentration. Maybe of contained violence. His massive muscles bunched as if ready to charge, and each placement of a fist on the ground looked like prep for brutality, like a warmup for the real thing.

And that was a good thing for the group of four's effort. Because the real thing was about to happen, and it all went down faster than Bodkin had ever pictured.

He and Gladdis Montrose had planned on an all-day mission, from dawn to dusk. Water supply in their hip packs, two protein bars each. Their usual. As it turned out, they wouldn't need to consume any of it, nor have time to.

The human hunters hung back as their enormous gorilla partner worked forward to the right, Sheba to the left. Montrose held a lightweight bolt-action rifle in her arms, one which she'd shot literally thousands of rounds through. Hopefully there'd be one, maybe two more well-placed shots with it today. Bodkin gripped his heavy, stainless steel .357 magnum, letting it hang down at ease. Hopefully no shots at all would be fired through it today. After Gladdis did her precision rifle work, it shouldn't be needed. Just a backup piece, as good in Bodkin's hands for bludgeoning as for shooting. The team of four ventured forth, the humans looking and listening, the beasts in front of them doing the same, plus scenting.

The location of Kagel's fruit and vegetable lures didn't look like much, and didn't stand out. Just a tiny clearing in the trees, the same as countless other clearings out here. Ragnor knew exactly where to go, however. After a gradual approach, with plenty of pauses to look around – forward, to the sides, to the rear, and of course up – they came upon the first baiting leftovers. Two burlap bags were lying twisted on the ground, moist, limp, and empty. One was still intact, the other torn apart. Maybe that bag contained some tasty morsels stuck in the burlap fibers, requiring some extra effort to remove them. Or maybe the creature thing, Tuma, was just being itself.

The wetland was a slowly awakening green paradise. Amongst the green glowed delicate red flowers of the Pine Lilly and hearty orange ones of the Butterfly weed. A songbird here and there, a slithering snake, a panicked little lizard ricocheting off the leafy twigs in front of them. But overall not much sound and very little movement in the wetland.

Mostly silent, seemingly peaceful.

Their stalk was but 27 minutes old, from the back gate of the compound's outdoor enclosure to the first baiting area, when the peaceful setting erupted.

Ragnor stopped dead, Sheba saw it and stopped as well. The dog turned her head just enough to see what Bodkin and Montrose were doing, and seeing them frozen in place, the dog turned back. She tilted her head up in the classic posture of a predator gathering maximum scents from the air. The wolf-dog breathed in deeply. Hair rose along the center of her back, and her body stiffened in readiness. At the same time, Ragnor huffed out loud, an exhalation of anger. Then the silverback gorilla took off.

To the nearest cypress tree, up its trunk, then a leap to the next tree, up another giant trunk. Ragnor scaled a fallen tree wedged between the current tree and yet another, then scrambled up a third trunk. Sheba followed the movements from underneath, watching her new ape partner's progress while watching for their quarry. Their prey may in fact have been near, but it couldn't yet be seen.

Montrose hustled to Sheba's right, moving through dense weeds without breaking stride. Bodkin did the same to the dog's left. Even though they searched primarily up in the trees, both kept one eye on the ground as well, in case of attack from there. Until the quarry's location was certain, all directions had to monitored.

Ragnor was over to a fourth tree, but this time the huge ape scrambled down a few feet from the present altitude. Bodkin assumed the gorilla was coming down, until he twisted around the trunk he was descending, gripping the bark in order to scale to its other side. To get to the other side…to whatever was there.

A bellow from Ragnor blasted through the swampland, and a screeching yelp answered it. Another ape appeared then: none other than Tuma.

Smaller than Ragnor but more agile, it attempted to flee, struggling on to a medium sized branch. It poised to leap away from the current tree, and Ragnor's bulk flew to it, clutching one of the other ape's legs.

The branch broke.

The two apes were for a split second airborne. One bulky and muscled, the other even more bulky and muscled, the bigger one still clinging to the smaller one's leg, despite the plunge. The two primates thumped to the muddy ground, making the swamp floor shake.

Up to their feet, standing, flailing arms, mouths agape with treacherous teeth bared, grunts and squeals ringing out. Ragnor wailing with furious hammer blows, Tuma with fists like a human boxer, moving forearms in a protective barrier, taking the blows of the gorilla there but saving its face and head. In this whirlwind of vicious motion, Sheba moved about, attempting a meaningful bite. After being slammed once by the body of each ape, Sheba staggered a moment. Tuma turned to engage the dog and whipped an uppercut to her jaw, sending her reeling in a daze. Tuma surged back to Ragnor, who had just slammed the killer ape's skull three times. Ragnor kept swinging.

Tuma met the attack. Block, block, jab, jab, then a knockout blow to the center of Ragnor's nose. For that instant, technique won over size and strength. Ragnor careened and dropped to the dirt in a furious heap, thrashing his arms and legs as he tried to get his bearing back.

Tuma had the chance to rush off, to escape. Sheba tried engaging it again, but the dog was now in a daze; Ragnor was back to his feet but reeling, hopping toward

Tuma and getting in the way of the clear shots for both armed hunters. Tuma started to leave, looked one last time at the hunters, then recognized Bodkin. As it looked into the human's eyes, Tuma's glare ignited with hatred. It was the stinking human again.

Kill it.

Tuma turned and rushed back toward them. It was afraid no longer. All four assailants were nothing to it. It led with a face that was one-third chimp, one-third gorilla, a tiny portion vampire bat and the rest murderous demon, focused on Bodkin as it advanced.

Montrose stepped forward with the rifle, iron sights coming up to zero in on a killing shot with no more thinking than a scorpion starting its sting. Sheba leapt to the ape's face, snapping at it but blocking that instant before Montrose squeezed the trigger.

Sheba had the ape's thumb in her mouth, and tore into it with razor teeth. Tuma screamed, and whipped Sheba's entire body like a boomerang straight into Montrose. Sheba and Montrose both tumbled and sprawled on the ground. Tuma rushed to annihilate both the wolf-dog and female huntress.

Bodkin was behind the ape freak, but he didn't dare shoot with Sheba and Montrose in the path just beyond the killer creature. A running jump, fillet knife in one hand, revolver in the other, onto the ape's back as it turned. The butt of the handgun slammed Tuma's forehead, Tuma clubbed Bodkin in the throat, Bodkin sliced the razor-sharp edge diagonal across Tuma's cheek bone.

A full-force battering ram hit Bodkin under the jaw, as the juggernaut of Tuma's body exploded into him, head to face. Down to the wet ground Bodkin went, shocked and without weapons.

Tuma instantly on top of him, clawing hands forming a huge hairy vice on either side of Bodkin's face. The mouth of the freak ape opened fully, baring long pointed teeth, formed by DNA partly ape but mostly bat. The face descended toward Bodkin's head.

Bodkin somersaulted back onto his own shoulders and head, trapping Tuma's right arm between his legs, his hands now gripping Tuma's furry wrist and twisting it into a position of non-strength. Bodkin then arched his back, straightening the killer ape's elbow in the most classic of all martial arts arm breaking techniques. Bodkin arched more, and he could hear connective tissue in Tuma's elbow start to go.

The ape stood with an agonized roar, picked its opponent clear up off the ground, and flung Bodkin into the greenery and mud. Tuma's elbow was now partly dislocated, that arm thus at only half strength. Tuma started toward the man-thing on the ground, this time with insane rage, determined to succeed in killing the human, no matter what else happened.

A massive dark limb, as wide as Tuma's head, encircled its neck. Ragnor picked the smaller ape up from its position on all fours, attempting to strangle his nemesis. Tuma flailed, found Ragnor's forearm, and bit in. Ragnor wailed and released Tuma, who still had Bodkin in focus.

A blonde missile hit Tuma from the side, Sheba biting into the ape's ribs. Tuma spun, and the dog released the ape's trunk and went for its throat. The dog was knocked back in midair, and Ragnor lunged forward to smash his foe again. Tuma absorbed a solid blow to the face, then neutralized Ragnor with a jab to the nose. Using its good arm.

In a blazing fury, Tuma turned and bounded up to and then on top of the male human, who had crawled several feet from where he'd been moments ago.

Tuma covered the human fully, grabbed the human's soft face with both hands, and opened its jaws wide, fangs ready for the fatal bite. Tuma started to strike downward, intending to sink its teeth into the victim's skull.

The strike stopped. Tuma tried to yank its head away from the human, away from the human's arm, from what was in the human's hand. But the ape couldn't, as the roof of its mouth was now stuck. Anchored on a hook of sorts.

It was held there by the small ridge of a revolver's stainless steel sight. The barrel of Bodkin's .357 magnum was in its mouth.

"Say 'Ahh'," Bodkin gasped.

FOOMP!

Tuma's body sat back up, as if electrified by the orange burst inside its mouth, by the muffled explosion of gunpowder. It's eyes stared ahead, now sightless, into the green paradise.

POW! POW!

Two eruptions popped on the side of Tuma's head, one below the ear and one just above it. The reports from the rifle Montrose held soared through the swamp for a moment. Then the wetland fell perfectly silent.

Tuma's limp, warm body fell off of Bodkin's midsection, away into a small patch of wetland wildflowers. Bodkin rolled away and leapt up, adrenaline cascading through every strand of bodily tissue. The revolver was still in his hand, but he knew he wouldn't need it at this point. Not considering where his slug had launched, and where Gladdis's bullets had landed. Three shots. Head. Head. Head. That usually ended things.

Sheba growled and approached the hot carcass; Bodkin grabbed her tail and yanked her back.

"Done. Good girl. Done," he said. She still growled and whined, agitated, considering a further rush. Bodkin crouched down, scooped her under the chest, and shoved the dog aside. That broke the spell. She slunk away and watched the dead ape from a distance.

"You OK, babe?" Bodkin said to Montrose, resting his hand on her shoulder. She nodded, attempted a smile, but it was strained, her eyes still possessed with battle.

"Must have been a comfy flight down for you," Bodkin said. "Your shots weren't off in the slightest."

"First class, bud. Only way to fly," Montrose said. Bodkin could hear tightness in her throat, a slight strangulation from the tension. They'd been here before. It would go away. Eventually.

"Wouldn't know. Never been on one yet," Bodkin said.

"I'll try to sneak you on some time," Montrose said.

Bodkin tried to answer that with a genuine smile, and almost made it. But there was that catharsis feeling when situations like this wound down, kind of an urge to cry or something. Always one of his greatest fears. No one, not even Gladdis, could ever see it break through. But if anything, Bodkin was a splendid actor.

"Maybe in one of those giant suitcases you lug to the check-in," he managed. The smile was almost a real one this time. He saw the sniper focus fading from her eyes as he smiled. She grinned back. Eyes now clearer, the beauty returning.

"In any case, we got the marauder. We definitely did," Montrose said, peering over at Tuma's body in the vegetation. She and Bodkin watched Ragnor in his enormity approach the other ape. The gorilla examined Tuma, as if curious. Or maybe sad.

"Unnaturally created," Bodkin said. "Brought into the world by no choice of its own. But it had to be done."

"Yep. The world's safer now. Hooray," Montrose said. "Hard to know if we should mourn, or if we should be happy."

The gorilla scooped up the fallen ape's head, lifting it off the ground. As if coddling it perhaps. At first, that's what it looked like.

Then Ragnor slammed the already dead head of Tuma down into the ground, immediately turning his back and maneuvering away, anger and disdain evident, as far as Bodkin could tell. And he guessed Ragnor's murdered wife was almost certainly the vision in the gorilla's mind.

The gorilla stood on two legs and pounded his chest, the staccato thumping like a long volley of machine gun fire. He shouted with his huge face looking skyward, screaming toward the treetops, to the heavens.

The wetland went silent again. The human hunters secured their firearms. Bodkin stroked Sheba's face for a moment, then he looked over at Montrose.

"If Ragnor's happy," Bodkin said. "Everybody's happy."

28

"Two first class tickets and five nights in the DoubleTree Royale in West Palm Beach…second week in January," Irwin Kagel said.

"Our friends at the United Nations won't question you on this?" Lee Bodkin said.

"How so?"

"Charging them for someone else's winter getaway, for starters."

"I travel when needed. For reasons crucial to research," Kagel said. He smirked in Bodkin's direction.

"The tickets and all being under the name of Gladdis Montrose won't raise any eyebrows?"

"No. She contracted for me. I've documented it all, and the project went swimmingly."

"Appropriate for Florida."

"It is. Only one concern in the whole endeavor. Her project was completed with a very questionable partner. A thug, sort of," Kagel said. "But a charming one. So the two of you are coming back down to the Sunshine State."

"I won't be here. I'll be either shivering in the Northwoods or in my woodworking shop in the garage. Gladdis will be heading down with someone else."

"A boyfriend?" Kagel said. Bodkin simply looked back at the researcher. "Um, well," Kagel said. "Is she looking forward to the next outing down in these parts?"

"Not sure. Actually, she doesn't know about the trip yet," Bodkin said. Kagel paused with that, but just for a few seconds.

"Mental health therapy, prescribed by Dr. Bodkin?"

"Uh, yeah. That has a certain ring to it. I like it."

"Why West Palm Beach?"

"A change of pace," Bodkin said.

"It wouldn't have anything to do with steering clear of Chicola, would it?"

"You're a man of deep insight, Doctor."

"So, never to return again."

"Gladdis won't. As for me, I have yet to catch one of your sea trout."

"The fish will be waiting for you. Where's your lovely lady partner now? If I may ask," Kagel said.

"On the beach with Sheba. Sleeping in the sun, last time I checked," Bodkin said.

"Is she safe? Out on the beach, asleep?" Kagel said.

"I just said, she's with Sheba."

The two men remained quiet for a moment, Kagel peering at Bodkin's face. The black eye had started to recede slightly, but now there was a bruise on his forehead, claw marks on his chin, and some kind of puncture on his cheek. Maybe macho man bounty hunting wasn't all it was made out to be. Kagel would stick to research for now.

"Oh, by the way, Lee. Tuma's body is in a holding area of the compound. In deep freeze storage."

"Excellent. The cops help you with the removal?" Bodkin said.

"No, I contacted one of the area gator hunting guides."

"The carcass of any use to you?"

"Oh yes. Dissection, analysis. Boring but important stuff. Hopefully I'll find some clues as to what we did wrong with his creation and treatments. But beyond that, the ape's parts will be invaluable for my malaria testing research."

"Wonderful. You mentioned the possibility of a living addition to the compound yesterday. Since the folks at the top learned of the Tuma risk factor being just a memory now."

"Yes. A wonderful female gorilla, bred in captivity. Excellent parents, sounds like," Kagel said.

"All gorilla?"

"Of course," Kagel said.

"No bat contributors?" Bodkin said.

Kagel looked at Bodkin, almost laughing, but the tragic reality too much to make light of. He just shook his head as he looked down.

"I had to shut my phone off," Bodkin said. "The voice mail's filled to capacity. Lots of reporters want answers from the team that tracked down the Panhandle Bigfoot."

"The media is calling it that?"

"They in fact are." Bodkin stood, reached his hand out, and Kagel shook it. "Take care, Irwin Kagel."

"How do I explain things? Is there a way to spin it?"

"Explain what? It was some kind of Sasquatch offshoot," Bodkin said. "From deep within the Florida swampland. Don't believe it, just ask the media."

"But what about when they finally get ahold of you? When you tell them about my experiment."

"What experiment?" Bodkin said. He opened the clinic's door, the Florida sun awaiting him outside.

Kagel digested that last statement. He was about to thank the other man, or express relief somehow.

Lee Bodkin stepped out, and the front door to the clinic popped shut.

P. J. Hafner is a St. Paul, Minnesota, native. Both an angler and bow hunter, he also spent 15 years as a wrestler and judo fighter, and is a repeat participant in the Twin Cities marathon and other running races. He's hiked in the Blue Ridge, Cascade, Chuckanut and Rocky Mountains, as well as in Switzerland and Iceland. Hafner holds degrees in English and Kinesiology.

He is also the author of *Stalk*, *Chuckanut Stalk*, *Marathon Stalk*, *Feast of the Badger*, and *Red Fang*.